Country Living,
Country Dying

Country Living, Country Dying

(A Witty Tale of Secrets Unburied)

by Able Jones

DOWN EAST BOOKS

Quotations in Chapter VIII from the essay "Spiritual Laws," by Ralph Waldo Emerson.

A note to the reader: Unfortunately, though the geography and weather may be familiar, no character in this book is based on anyone real—living, dead, or otherwise.

ISBN 0-89272-378-5
Library of Congress Catalog Card Number 95-83130

Printed and bound at Capital City Press, Montpelier, Vt.

2   4   6   8   9   7   5   3   1

Cover illustration by Anita Crane

Jacket design by Lurelle Cheverie

Book design by Carolyn Lockwood

Down East Books • Camden, Maine 04843

*"The village, unlike the supermarket, was
territory still well known. . . ."*

—*Dick Francis,* Comeback

Cast of Characters

BUZZ NOBLE, bachelor, native, and dump manager

DOG, his dog

ADELE TRUE, who lives alone and owns a gift shop in the village

GLINDA TRUE, her cousin, who lives away and returns for a visit

EDNA and MERTON TRUE (Gram and Gramps), Adele and Glinda's grand-parents, who raised both girls

REVEREND ALOYSIUS KILDARE, retired Episcopal priest, who moved to town twenty years ago

EDWARD MONTGOMERY — "SNOOKY" — Fr. Kildare's companion and housekeeper

HAROLD MOSBY, mute, who lives in his '73 Chevy

GERALD TIBBETS, County Deputy and Emergency Medical Technician

SGT. LIAM CELTED, a Boston police detective

JOHN STANDISH DIDDLES — "PUCK" — native, man about town, vinyl siding and home improvement salesman

WILMA LOOK, librarian at Town Library

MR. GUNTHER KRINGLE, foreign businessman and town benefactor

OLGA, Mr. Kringle's "cousin"

Marc, a fitness salon instructor; Julia Child; Jason, Snooky's San Francisco cousin; Yvonne Tibbets, Gerald's wife; Clyde, Milton, Ginny, and other folks at the Store; the Coors/Doritos delivery man; the Ladies of the Fire Auxiliary; various policemen; and other characters who compose the town and the story.

Fido, Adele's Maine coon cat; Pussums, Snooky's Dandie Dinmont terrier; Olga's dog; and other pets.

Earth Angel, the town's backhoe; Henry Ford, a truck; Harold Mosby's '73 Chevy; the Mercedes truck; the hearse, etc.

SETTING: present day in the village of Bosky Dells, Maine. Incorporated in 1784, the village of Bosky Dells is nestled in the unspoiled lake region in the wooded hills of mid-central Maine, a little off the beaten track. Pop. 827.

Preface

If you like scarlet, magenta, hot pink, bright orange, and greeny brass against cloudless and unfailing baby blue, then September was glorious. Cool in the mornings, hot by noon, misty at night, and hardly a day of rain. Colorful, too.

Business thrived in the little towns scattered among the Maine hills. The leaves turned right on schedule, and car- and bus-loads of leafers came to see them. The cars and busses stopped at the country stores, gift shops, scenic overlooks, roadside tables, and at the gas stations known for their clean facilities. The leafers bought soda and coffee and seafood-salad rolls and postcards and aspirin and small stuffed animals and log-cabin balsam-incense burners and cranberry soap and local honey and country-style Christmas decorations. A bumper sticker that read WELCOME TO MAINE, NOW GO HOME was a great seller, especially among people from New Jersey. The leafers said: "what a good town to visit" and "aren't the leaves just fantastic?" and added how "lucky" the clerk was to live here year-round, and that they were seriously thinking of "retiring to a place just like this someday." Then they got back in their car or bus and left.

The Smokey the Bear sign at the edge of town read TODAY'S FIRE DANGER: HIGH for many weeks. Then the rain began the middle of October. The first night's wind brought down the pretty leaves. Next morning each tree stood in a puddle of scarlet, magenta, hot pink, and bright orange, as though it had dropped its ruffled party dress around its ankles. The leaves that remained turned silvery and lavender—much easier on the eye, though no good for the pocketbooks. Most trees stood like dark skeletons in the drenching rain. "Wouldn't you know it," said someone at the Store, "just when things were looking up for a change."

It didn't stop raining. Woodpiles got soaked, basements filled up, announcements posted in the Store's front window bled in the damp and steamy air. Everyone complained. Several back roads washed out. Cows stood in the rain and watched the repair work. Apples got stem rot; cabbages still in the ground turned to mush.

Up at the town dump, it's likely that the silver purse showed up first. One corner emerged from the grit of the old landfill, then probably the whole thing. It rained some more and the purse was washed clean, and to any passerby (though in that abandoned section of the dump, no one passed by) it would look as though it had recently been dropped on the cinders.

The rain didn't let up, and next the tips of the radius and ulna were exposed and washed clean; then the five metacarpals. The first and second phalanges would have emerged next, but the rain stopped, the sun came out, and everyone cheered up. There would be a little break before the deer hunters arrived, a little break during which the town belonged to the people who lived there year-round. A break, and probably some beautiful Indian summer days, too.

Chapter 1

In Which the Town of Bosky Dells Begins
To Celebrate Hallowe'en

Dog crossed the street. Nothing much doing in the little New England hamlet of Bosky Dells, as it was early and the citizens still abed. He sniffed the smoldering remains of a rubber tire, chased a rat for half a block, though strictly speaking there were no blocks, and nibbled—but did not swallow—the slabs of broken pumpkin that littered the street. Toilet paper, hanging in shreds from the last remaining stately elm, blew gently in the morning breeze. Dog lay down in front of the Store to await opening time.

One by one, up and down the short streets that ended abruptly in woods, puffs of smoke announced that breakfast fires were being lit against the chill of late October. Dog waited. Most dogs in town had names—Nipper, Gonzo, Dylan, Brownie, Blackie, Whitie, Pussums. Why didn't he?

For the reason that he more or less belonged to Buzz Noble, dump manager, who had a dread of naming things he loved.

Buzz gave several good reasons for this. His great-great-grandfather's farm had burnt to the ground. This was many years ago; still, everyone talked about it sometimes, and recalled that it had been torched, some thought, and still said. Once that farm had a name. Buzz knew it, though he would not say it. Just about everyone he'd ever loved was dead, and if you were to think about it, they all had names. Buzz had named his first truck "Henry Ford," One fall night, she lost her brakes and plummeted down Milk Mill Hill Road and out onto the glare ice on 27, where she spun around, slid into a deep ditch, and landed on two mating moose. Buzz was not hurt, the moose limped away, but Henry Ford was pretty much totaled. That incident changed Buzz's thinking forever.

For this and other reasons, Buzz had never married or had children. "Dog" was one thing, Buzz always said, but "Wife," "Boy," "Girl," that would've been real odd. Someone always chuckled and said, "Aw Buzz, stuff a sock in it." But it made Buzz nervous when "the dump," where he had worked his entire life, got the name of "Transfer Station." Of course everyone went on calling it "the dump," but the new sign at the entrance said "Transfer Station." To Buzz, this changed everything, and he lived in dread that some untoward doom would someday befall his workplace. He spent many anxious hours brooding on what that might be, and scanning the sky at all seasons of the year while he dug at the garbage and tended his rubbish fires and sorted through the trash. Portents often appeared of something that felt like disaster, he thought, especially in autumn when the required polyethylene bags often broke under the weight of sharp animal bones inside, some of them with the fur still clinging.

Buzz sometimes wished he had a normal religion. But having long ago abandoned his Baptist upbringing, such as it was, and now unable to join any organization, especially one with a name, his mind was adrift in a gnostic sea of private imaginings. Somewhat like Dog's.

Father Kildare, a kindly man, who had retired to Bosky Dells twenty years ago along with Snooky, a former chorister and now (for almost forty years, if truth be told) Father Kildare's cook and companion, had taken pity on Buzz. On his and Snooky's weekly trip to the dump, Father Kildare had often urged Buzz to come by for a talk, or to attend the monthly Bible study-cum-sherry-cum-ecumenical prayer night in what Snooky called "the second best parlor," but, to no avail. With the exception of Dog, and one or two of his Indian friends, Buzz felt he had to face his questions alone.

The morning mist was rising and life was stirring. From Up Street came the sound of a chain-saw refusing to catch hold. A truck left town, grinding its gears. Harold Mosby, who lived in his '73

Chevrolet, pale blue, without tires, parked in a little grove of trees near the lake, opened the passenger's-side door, the only one that still worked, came out into the chill pleasant morning, and stretched. The Coors/Doritos delivery truck pulled up to the closed Store and the driver, realizing he too had a wait, opened his back door, slipped out a cold one, and wearily opened a bag of sour-cream ranch-type with low-salt and Jalapeños. He threw a few to Dog, who ate them gratefully.

Because he had no name, Dog was not often called to get some dinner, so he tended to eat whatever came his way, though he had never developed a taste for burnt inner tube or raw pumpkin. A potato chip for breakfast, however, could be a pretty good thing. The hippies who ran the sacred oil factory, just about the town's only industry, "Patchouli & All," began early-morning flute practice, and all across downtown the patient and not unattractive strains of a raga wafted; it might look to some nature-loving tourist as though the toilet paper in the big elm moved in graceful response.

Dog scratched. Harold Mosby scratched and headed towards the Store for some breakfast. The Coors delivery man sat in the front of his truck, smoking, eating his chips, and drinking his beer. By now, folks were up and about. Snooky, for example, was in his kitchen coddling himself an egg in a tiny knob of butter, a spoon of heavy cream, a sprinkle of bouquet garni, and a grind of white pepper. Somewhere, in the mist, a horn got stuck. Someone turned on a radio to a rock station. The Store owner arrived, unlocked the door, entered, and turned on the neon lights and the blue BUD LITE sign in the window. The Coors man stubbed out his cigarette, shoved the can underneath the seat, jumped down and opened his side door, and pulled out a big rack of chips. Various vehicles pulled in—the early-morning newspaper, coffee, and gossip crowd. The postmaster came down from his apartment over the post office with an American flag under his arm, attached it to a short pole, unlocked the door, and went inside.

At the same moment, Adele True, a sturdy middle-aged lady

dressed in pieces of brown and gray, came out the front door of her house across from the Store, down her granite steps, looked to the left and the right, crossed the street, walked up a gravel path, up some wooden steps, reached into her pocket, took out her key ring, and unlocked the door of her herb, pottery, and general gift shop, "About Thyme," which was sandwiched in between the Store and the post office. It was Saturday, she sighed to herself, as well as Hallowe'en. October—not a good month for tourists, at least not this late. Nothing much doing now until pre-Christmas, but she may as well open up anyhow, maybe dust a few things, drag some Christmas stuff up from the root cellar, unpack it, see if the mice had made nests with the tinsel.

In short, it was a town that locked up at night, unlocked in the morning, on a regular basis. Cardboard signs on strings flipped to CLOSED and then to OPEN, but everyone knew the hours to get mail, buy meat, have coffee, see what was happening. Small goods and small money changed hands. Various commodities (beer, potato chips, people, stray dogs) entered the town, got churned around in some way or other, and left it again as returnable empties, as trash to the dump, as tourists, as philosophers. It looked like the beginning of a warm, sunny, normal day.

Adele had three customers, a man and two women, who wanted maple-sugar candy in the shape of Santa. Adele said she'd certainly have them later in the season. Disappointed, they bought a breadboard in the shape of a loon and a bag of horehound drops. They asked to use the bathroom, but Adele didn't have one in the shop. After they left, she rearranged the breadboards and looked for a catalog of wooden toys, but did not find it. She counted the mittens and dusted the bicentennial pottery mugs. Exactly at 11:30, she flipped her OPEN sign to GONE FOR LUNCH and left for home. She unlocked her front door, entered the dark hallway, and slipped on an envelope lying on the floor under the mail slot. Odd. For one thing, she usually picked up her mail at the post office. Must be the new weekend clerk's fault. For another, she seldom got letters. And pink? A pink envelope? She took it out to the kitchen, put it on the table, filled her kettle for tea, rummaged in the refrigerator for some lunch. First things first, and food was important.

Only when she'd made her cup of Lapsang Souchong and found half a can of corned beef and made some rye toast, did she sit down, pick up a clean knife, and slit open the square pink envelope. The handwriting was unfamiliar, but the letter began "My dear cousin"

> My dear cousin,
>
> Surprised, I bet! Well, it's me! After all this time! Just a short note to say hello and to say I've decided to pay the old home-town and you a little visit. I know it's been a long time! Who would believe it! But now just seems like a good time to visit. I've got vacation time coming, will drive up in my new car. Oh, guess I should say when. Well, I and my best friend Tina went to this tea-shop where this woman reads your tea leaves just for fun? Of course neither Tina nor I takes things like this serious, but the woman did say I'd meet a tall dark and handsome, which as a matter of fact I did, will tell you all when arrive, and also that I'd be taking a journey on Samhain. Well! So I'll be arriving there late on Samhain! I'd like the old guest room, okay. Needless to say, I am looking really forward to seeing you after all these years. Must close. So until then.
>
> Love, your cousin G.

Adele began to shake. She sucked her lips, pulled her sweater tight around her, felt sweaty. On the stove, the kettle began to scream and boil over. She rushed to grab it. This news, she said to herself, calls for a spoon of rum in my tea. But she changed her mind, returned to the table, and reread the letter. Could this be true? Was this a joke? Was this Glinda's handwriting after all these years? Adele held it up to the window, read it again. Glinda coming for a visit? Coming back after all these years? Coming back, after all those promises never to set foot in town again, ever? Glinda, who had already ruined Adele's life once? And laughed about it, too. Adele could still feel that laugh.

Sucking her tea, trembling, sweating, mopping up a spill with the wristband of her tan sweater-coat, Adele stared out the kitchen window at the blue, blue noon sky.

She could see the front porch of About Thyme, and that some tourists had stopped and were peering in the front windows. Then they were laughing at the name of the shop, pointing to the hand-painted sign over the porch. Then some of them were posing under the sign, and another was pointing a camera. Adele thought of running across the street to open up, but decided she was too upset. I'll read the letter again. They probably wouldn't buy anything, anyway.

Try to take in the details. She skimmed it, tried to slow down. All this talk of love and missing, she didn't believe a word of it. And this weird word, "Samhain." What was that? Trust Glinda to get cute, not say "next Wednesday" or "Monday afternoon" like ordinary people. Adele was not the least bit concerned about following orders and getting the guest room off the kitchen ready. Just like Glinda to start making demands, before she even got here. No, Adele was concerned about herself, about the threat, about being strong enough. I've gotten spoiled after all this time, she thought. Let down my armor. At least give me a day or two to get used to the idea. That is, if this is a genuine letter. Which did not solve the problem, as the clock ticked on, of when was this "Samhain."

Who would know? The laughing people were getting back in their car, without having bought one bag of potpourri, one pottery votive-candle holder, one card with pressed flowers, one potholder with sea gulls or pine trees. So much for making any money this afternoon, Adele grieved. Snooky! Snooky knows things. He'll know.

Feeling a little fortified, Adele got up to use the wall phone. Fitting her trembling forefinger in the slightly greasy holes, she at last managed to dial the Rectory phone. (Even though Father Kildare was long retired, and "The Rectory" was not and never had been a rectory at all, he was fond of the name and had christened the house as soon as he'd bought it. Nearly the week he and Snooky had moved in, he had come to Adele's shop and ordered two hand-painted signs from a catalog. One, in "Olde Englishe Script" for over the front door that said "Est. 1901," and another, also in "Olde Englishe Script" to be fixed to a post out front that said "The Rectory."

Everyone in town had laughed at this, openly, because "1901" wasn't the date of the house at all, as they all knew very well, but 1801 or "even older, for sure," some said. But they didn't let on to Father Kildare, and if he couldn't read what was written on the page of a perfectly good deed, he didn't need them to tell him any different. They also all knew that Charlie Sirois the real estate salesman had only been able to sell the house to Father Kildare because of lying about the date. As the town owned the house, everyone believed that its sale would fatten the town coffers and reduce taxes, too.

Charlie had been able to get rid of the house, empty for so many years, by assuring Father Kildare and Snooky that "she's not that old and if she's held up this good for *nearly* a hundred years, she'll hold up good for some more." Both Father and Snooky had a dread of fixing anything and, of course, neither could. They did admire "patina" however, which Charlie Sirois assured them was not real but "antiqued." "Took a lot," Charlie kept saying, "to get her to look a lot older than she really is! Amazin', ain't it?" Everyone enjoyed this story, though now and then one of the listeners would wonder whether or not Father Who's-it or "that danged houseboy of his" would ever discover the "secret room" in which they were sure there had once been witch rites and witch trials in "the olden days." Then someone always added that if the preacher or his little friend there ever pressed the secret panel and plunged into that secret room with God knows what ancient date carved into the woodwork someplace, it'd be all up with Charlie Sirois, and the While a While Real Estate Company would for sure get sued. The pleasure of watching—or just even hearing about—Charlie in trouble also delighted the coffee drinkers and storytellers, and in this state of mixed emotions they managed to keep the Mr. Coffee perking with free refills.)

Ring, ring, ring. Adele knew Snooky was home because from her kitchen window she could see him rushing around in his kitchen next door. She could see smoke inside the room. Ring, ring, ring.

Drats, she thought. Finally she could see Snooky fling his hands into the air, wipe them on his apron , and lunge in the direction of the phone.

"Oh Lord *yes*, what *can* I do for *you*?" came the high, exasperated, but always comforting Snooky voice, accompanied by a crashing of lids, cooking spoons, the motor of the Cuisinart, the instructional voice of a cooking show on the breakfast nook TV, and a bark from Pussums, the terrier.

"Snooky," said Adele, "are you busy right this minute?"

"Precious," replied Snooky, who loved an interruption as well as he loved his neighbors, especially Adele. "Precious! Busier than Buzz on dump day, but *do* go on!" Looking from her kitchen into his kitchen, Adele could see him turn off the front burners, flick off the Cuisinart, put the TV on hold, and flip a towel (and a slippered foot) at Pussums. All was quiet.

"Snooky," said Adele, trying to keep her voice normal, "I need to know a little something, and I thought you were the one who would know."

"Darling, ask on," said Snooky, kicking Pussums into the front hallway and slamming the door.

"Snooky," said Adele carefully, "what is 'Samhain,' do you think?"

"Let me guess. Some kind of, oh God, new brand of that nasty low-cal marg?"

"No," said Adele, "I don't think so. I think it's the name of some kind of date."

"Date? Darling, as in date bars? as in Christmas pud? as in stuffed?"

"No, I don't think so. I think, as in calendar type of date, you know, as in event?"

"Lord," said Snooky, "wait a sec." And Adele could see him fling a smoking pan into his sink, whereupon steam lapped over the window and she could see no more. Seconds ticked by.

"Love," exclaimed Snooky, out of breath, "You have *no* idea what it's like to fix lunch for this man! Now, what were you saying?"

"Samhain, Samhain, but I'm not sure how to pronounce it. When is it? Part of Christmas or something?"

"Hmmm. Samhain. Precious, I think I've heard that before, but let me go ask the old Slave Driver," and with that, Snooky flung down the phone. Again, seconds passed, then minutes. Adele could hear Pussums bark, could hear shouts, could hear a door slam, a door open, more shouts, what sounded like a heavy book hitting wood, then yelping.

"Darling. Sorry!" said Snooky, even more out of breath. "The Padre combed what's left of his sotted brains and *thinks* it was yesterday. Is that possible? Some ancient cult event. Something like him!" (Snooky tittered at his own humor.) "An old name for Hallowe'en, or the day after maybe, something like that. Or did he mean today? I mean, things get so ballsy out here in the sticks what with all the work I've got to do constantly, and with the boys celebrating holidays any old time they feel like burning a tire or playing with potty paper so I hardly know if today is Hallowe'en or tomorrow, or is today the eve of tomorrow, or what? God, my mind in these rustic circumstances! Anyhow, Darling, I hope that's helpful because I'm certainly at this point not planning on speaking to *him* for the rest of the day. Why did you want to know? Having a special sale or something?"

Meantime, Adele's blood has sunk to her feet. She snatched up the letter and glanced through it once more. Samhain. If Samhain was yesterday, then Glinda was late. And Glinda, no matter how insane and inconsiderate and selfish she may have been or still was, was never ever late getting anywhere, not even to the dentist or something like that. Obviously, she was supposed to have been here last night. And obviously, she was not.

"Yam, ah, yes," she said into the phone, "yes, Snooky, that's it. A sale. I knew you'd know. Thanks so much. See you soon." Which is how Adele and Snooky always said good-bye. But as for "seeing him soon," she could see him right now, rescuing his burnt pan, turning his TV back on, and wiping his hands again on his striped cook's apron. At least, Adele thought, slowly hanging up the sweaty phone, at least there's always Snooky. And she sat down in her chair again, lifted her cold cup of tea, and began to worry where could Glinda be.

Chapter II

An Unexpected Trick, Not Treat,
Turns Up at the Town Dump

It had been a very good week for Buzz at the dump. The weeks before Christmas were always especially good ones. Buzz figured that it had something to do with the holiday. In anticipation of the onslaught of gifts and new things, or cleaning to get ready for relatives or somebody, people scoured their corners and closets, making room for ever bigger and newer piles of junk, all of which, Buzz knew, would eventually end up at the dump, some year or other. Fair pickings for himself, and Dog.

This week, in fact, had been so good that he was planning a trip up north to the Indian reservation. The Indians were Buzz's best customers for two reasons. One, they really liked the stuff he brought up—old Elvis lamps, rusty ice skates, dead naugahyde chairs (lime green was best), iceboxes with rounded corners, assorted car parts, especially steering wheels. Two, they lived far enough away from Bosky Dells that the stuff never reappeared as "antiques" and "collectibles" at the Better Late Than Never store on Dibble Road.

Buzz's great grandmother had been one-fourth Indian, and Buzz liked to tell people who didn't know better that he was a "large part Indian" himself. He wasn't exactly sure to which tribe his great-grandmother had belonged, but to his thinking, it didn't matter that much. Indian was Indian. At any rate, he felt a certain camaraderie with the residents of Indian Flats, and about once every two months would load the dump's dump truck with his scavenged treasures, slip a Conway Twitty tape into his Walkman, tweet for Dog, and head north on what he called "that lonesome highway."

The dump's dump truck was another reason that Buzz liked to travel every few months or so. It was a 1967 Mercedes, red, with real leather seats, and an engine that still purred like a panther. Next to Henry Ford, Buzz considered it the best truck ever made, and he maintained it in the best condition. Twenty-something years ago, the Mercedes had been a gift to the town from the only German immigrant—Buzz thought just about the only immigrant from any-place; everyone else was from here—Mr. Gunther Kringle, who had appeared sometime after the war, bought a house, and settled into a solitary, off and on, and mysterious existence. Kringle would be gone for long periods of time. Worse, he didn't explain where he went or who he was or what he did. He didn't hang out at the Store in the morning. Some people said he didn't even shop there at all.

Sometimes Kringle had company that drove up to see him in big, dark cars with out-of-state plates. Someone reported having seen a man who "looked just like Hitler" fleeing from the house into a long black car and speeding away into the night, not once but several times, but no one paid a bit of attention to this story. "Yeah, sure, and there were German submarine boats on the beach at Jonesport, too," someone always said. "It's all right to mind your own business," someone else said, "but at least you ought to tell folks what it is." To this wisdom, everyone did agree. The last mys-terious thing Kringle did was give the town the red Mercedes truck. No one knew if it was on purpose or by accident that it was deliv-ered the day of his funeral, three days after he committed suicide (for mysterious reasons) in what is now Snooky's front parlor. When Snooky heard this story, he almost refused to move into the house, though he had to admit it was a steal, and a perfect location, and in good repair for such an old, old place.

On the day of Kringle's funeral, just as they were lowering him down into his solitary plot, what should come grinding and purring down the cemetery road but Kringle's gift, shiny, new, red, with a big sign on the bumper reading "To the good citizens of Bosky Dells from G. Kringle. Keep on dumping," and the Mer-cedes dealer from South Portland driving it all the way. The town not only got the truck but the house and its contents as well, as no next of kin or even a business partner or lawyer or distant cousin or anybody ever showed up to claim it or explain Kringle's life and death. The house stood empty until Father Kildare and Snooky bought it, some years after Kringle's sad end.

Buzz had fallen in love with the red truck the first moment he saw it, and he vowed, as he stood at the edge of the cemetery watching the funeral, that someday he would become dump manager instead of dump assistant, and would get to drive it himself.

On this last day of October, Buzz was looking forward to his trip to Indian Flats. He had the whole front end of a Camaro already loaded, and was struggling with a swing set when, out of the corner of his eye, he caught the glint of something shiny lying a ways off. With his practiced eye, he could tell this was not a tin can or a piece of aluminum siding, and he hurried over to inspect it. Squatting down alongside the silvery thing, he farted loudly. Luckily, when he glanced about in guilty fashion, no one but Dog was in sight. Buzz felt better, and once again bent over the shiny thing on the pile of debris.

The shards of pumpkin had by now been run over many times and were flattened, smeared, and drying on the street in front of the Store. The day had turned a little gray. About Thyme remained closed for the afternoon, an unprecedented occurrence that nevertheless went unnoticed by any local. Adele stayed home, was taking a fitful nap on the horsehair sofa in the cold front room. Fido, her coon cat, slept at her feet, but it was hard because Adele had not removed her brogues and often put a thick sole into Fido's sleeping side. Nevertheless, Adele slept on, and Fido slept on, the clock ticked in the kitchen, the faucet dripped a little, and the old house creaked and moaned in the afternoon wind.

The Store was quiet because the coffee drinkers and lunch crowd had at last dispersed to their own homes (or car, in the case of Harold Mosby), and whatever tourists came through town saw Adele's GONE FOR LUNCH sign and drove to the next town over where the gift shop was open 24 hours a day, including Christmas.

Snooky had thrown a dish towel over the dirty lunch plates,

ripped off his apron in a huff, tearing out one of its strings, and sat down to sulk in his kitchen rocking chair. At his feet, Pussums crunched on the burnt remains of lunch from a Wedgwood plate, which Snooky had given him in spite. Usually, Pussums ate from a pottery dish that said PUSSUMS on the side, and ordinarily, Snooky would have killed anyone who put a piece of his Wedgwood on the floor, much less get dog germs on it. But Snooky was having a snit, and darkly entertaining the thought of packing his bags, making arrangements with Adele to send on his Wedgwood, his Julia Child videos, his copper saucepans, while he took the bus to Boston and then Amtrak cross-country (he had it all figured out, and would rather die than fly) to San Francisco where his cousin Jason lived and owned a posh little gallery called "Next Door" which was next door to a posh little bar called "Henry Orient."

Jason threw little soirees for openings at which friends stood about eating things and admiring, discussing, and sometimes buying each other's art work. Jason had often pleaded with Snooky to come out, live with him in his airy big old place, and cook little things for the gallery parties, and do what *Snooky* wanted to do for a change. "Really!" Jason would say, "Snooky! When do you intend to start living your own life?" (A not very moot question, as Snooky had just about already done that.)

Ah, well (following this always comforting fantasy of revenge, packing, leaving, serving people right, and so forth), Snooky thought, ah well, patting his hair into place, I am certainly much too exhausted to pack right this minute. Whereupon he nodded off with half an eye on the clock for how much longer the veal cutlets could safely marinate in olive oil, a dash of bitters, a branch of rosemary. He slept; Pussums slept; Father Kildare slept; at her house, Adele slept; Harold Mosby snored a bit in his front seat. All the clocks ticked on. Bosky Dells took a much needed nap, considering the long night to come.

All except for Buzz who was digging with his stubby fingers at the shiny thing which, it turned out, was not lying on top of the debris but somehow stuck in it, or sunk in it, and actually seemed to be attached to something not yet visible.

Buzz scratched for awhile, then went to the truck and fished around under the front seat for a large metal spoon with a very short, charred handle which had turned up in the bag of trash Snooky had left last week. Going through the bag after Snooky left (the most interesting things often turned up in the trash from the Rectory), Buzz had seen the spoon and figured it would come in handy. Spoon in hand, Buzz trotted back to his digging. After a few minutes, he began to realize that the shiny thing was bigger than he thought, and not any kind of flattened can or, in fact, anything that he much recognized, until he had finally scraped all around it and it came to him that it was a woman's pocketbook, silver, leather! Crinkly leather, too! Jeez, thought Buzz, silver alligator! Are them Indian ladies gonna love this!

He dug a bit further around where the handle ought to be and suddenly unearthed some old chicken bones. Shit, Buzz thought, probably ruined the purse gettin' buried in with some dead chicken. He scraped and scraped and scraped up a bone with . . . what? A chicken bone with a ring on it? A ring around it? Buzz looked closer. A green ring. An emerald?

He fell back on his heels, and after remaining silent for a time, said aloud, "Jesus, Mary, and Joseph. Holy Shit. Whaaa?" as he realized he had seen that ring before. And he knew who had been wearing it. And it had been no chicken. And he could remember thinking he thought he knew where she had gotten it, and when. And why, for that matter. And who from. He remembered her holding her hand up and turning the ring so it caught the light from the drive-in's screen and saying "OOO, Buzz, is this a pretty thing or what?" And, though the crew cut on his neck stood straight up in the autumn air, and the taste of vomit was in his throat, Buzz reached into the little hole he had dug and gently put his dirty hand around the slender wrist he remembered so well.

He was sweating, but he was also shivering. Naw, he thought, this is crazy. She's been gone for years. She's not been around these parts for years. She went on years ago to bigger and better things than this here. And me. Check the pocketbook. Using the edge of Snooky's cooking spoon, Buzz pried open the rusted jaws of the silver purse. The contents were faded, dirty, matted. A stuck tube of "Lilacs in the Snow" (he read on the bottom); he pulled and tugged at the cap and finally it came off to reveal a melted nub of purple, a purple he remembered the look of, the taste of, the difficulty of removing from a shirt front before his mother saw it. Shit, he said again, replacing the cap and carefully laying the lipstick on the ground. He reached in again and pulled out a set of rusty keys, none of which he recognized, though they had a "G" hanging from the ring. He placed those on the ground. A comb was next, with a few broken teeth and a few light, long hairs. What was once a white card. Buzz turned it over. "You Have an Appointment with Your Dentist on May 2, 1967 at 12:15 P.M. If You Cannot Keep This Appointment, Please Inform Our Office 24 Hours Ahead of Time."

Jeez, thought Buzz, that's a long time ago. And he put the card on the ground next to the lipstick, the keys, the comb. And, shaking, reached for the wallet. But he knew what it would contain—the "G" word—and, it did. On a Grant's layaway card. On a beautician's license card. On an Elvis fan club card. Some damp dollar bills, all stuck together. A folded piece of paper with some, looked like, telephone numbers. He pulled out the last thing in the purse—a ticket, he thought. He unfolded it, spread it out as best he could on his filthy knee. A Greyhound ticket, unused, one-way to Boston for May 3, 1967, lv. 3:29 P.M. arr. Boston 9:27 P.M. For a fleeting minute, he wondered if it was still good, on account of he'd always wanted to go south for a while. But he had this crazy thought because he was in shock and as soon as he had the thought he came to his senses, and looked into the hole and at the slender wrist, now a handful of bones, and knew beyond the shadow of any possible doubt whose wrist he now held once more in his sweaty, shaky fingers.

A little after four o'clock, Harold Mosby crawled out of his Purple Haze sleeping bag and emerged from the door of his '73 Chevy. He yawned, stretched, grunted, ran his fuzzy tongue over his six or so teeth, and went into the bushes to pee. With a full bladder, as he had now, he was able to write his whole name— Harold, Phinneas, Washington, Mosby—in the brown, dry leaves lying on the yellowed ground. This accomplished, he went back to his car and carefully straightened his purple sleeping bag.

He was very proud of his sleeping bag. It was also very warm. It had been a Christmas present from the town six years ago when it became apparent that Harold, who after all came from an old family, had no intention of moving out of his '73 Chevy and into a halfway house or someplace like that where, said some newcomers, somebody like him belonged.

Puck Diddles was Second Selectman and Overseer of the Poor that year, and he said he thought Harold should be left alone, but that he was eligible for assistance. "He's got money," said the Third Selectman. "He owns that whole goddamn side of the lake; he's just so goddamn stubborn that's where he wants to live." "Well, we can't allow him to freeze his ass to death," said the First Selectman, "stubborn or not." Puck Diddles suggested they use some assistance funds to buy Harold a sleeping bag at the Army Surplus. But it was the good folks from the sacred oil factory, who were still into Jimi Hendrix, who suggested the Purple Haze down bag instead. Warmer, they claimed; plus purple, which would enhance Harold's self-image. Puck said, below his breath, "Fuck that," but nevertheless approved the expenditure, especially as the sacred-oil-factory folks offered to go to Freeport and pick out the bag and bring it back. Like everything else, the story got around town. Some citizens thought Harold did not need a $400 sleeping bag, taxes being what they were. But, it was Christmas, so the grumbling soon settled down.

Aside from the fact that Harold liked the color of his bag, and liked getting a surprise, and also liked staying warm inside it, every time he looked at it he could feel his secret. Everyone in town thought the sleeping bag was his most valuable possession (next to owning the lake frontage), but Harold knew better. No one but Harold knew what he had in the trunk of his car. No one could have guessed that in the trunk of his car, and wrapped in a piece of red blanket, was someone he could talk to. It was his treasure, his precious, his royal jewel. For, tucked in that scrap of blanket was his 1911 Honus Wagner mint condition baseball card, with Honus Wagner's smiling but serious face on it. Harold talked things over with Honus, and Honus always listened.

When Harold was eleven, his father, whom he had never met before, at least not that he could recall, had shown up on the doorstep of the old Mosby place and asked to see "my boy." Everyone in the house, including the woman Harold called "Mom,"—or rather, called her that in his head—objected, but finally let Harold leave the house with his father. They went to lunch at the lunch counter in what was then called "General Store & Farm Supply," the same store where Harold now eats breakfast and lunch, but which is now called "Country Corner" and of course it's all a lot more fixed up than it used to be.

"I ain't here to say I'm sorry I ain't been around to raise ya'," Phinneas told Harold. "I don't wanna come draggin' back at this point with a big story. No, I don't. By the looks of ya', the doctor was right and ya' weren't worth raisin' anyhow. Course I am some sorry 'bout you gettin' kicked by that horse, when I had ya' out in the barn there. Likely, I should of told your mom about it, but ya' weren't bleedin' or nothing, and I figured you to be okay. Guess not. Never said a word again, didja? Too bad. Well, there's worse. Might be I was wrong on that one, though. Don't matter now. I ain't ever plannin' to see ya' again. Got a real big job offer, outta state. But I figgered I owed ya' sompin'."

With that, Phinneas handed Harold the baseball card wrapped in a waxed paper sandwich bag. "Here, boy, take this. My legacy to ya'. Keep it till you're old and gray. Or, if ya' ever git hard up, you can take it to somebody with money and see what it's worth. Just be sure they know what they're doin'."

Phinneas had paid the $3.25 lunch bill for himself and his son, bought a box of wooden toothpicks and a cream soda, and left town for the last time. Harold wrapped the card in a little scrap of red blanket, then in a box, and then hid it under his bed.

One night, many years later—maybe he'd already moved into

his car, he couldn't remember for sure—he'd gotten real hungry. He dug the blanket out of the trunk and took the card and crept up to Mr. Gunther Kringle's kitchen door and knocked. Harold pressed his ear against the door and could hear scuffling of some kind, some muttering, but presently footsteps and the door opened and Mr. Kringle peered out into the moonlight.

"Vat? Who is there?"

Harold extended his hand with the card in it. Mr. Kringle growled, took it, lifted his glasses up on his forehead, held the card up to the porch light. He turned the card in his hand, and finally handed it back to Harold.

"Very nice, Harold. Vort tousands, someday. Take care of it." And he closed the door.

This transaction did not alleviate the grumbling of Harold's stomach, but he figured that Mr. Kringle had money and so Mr. Kringle would know. He took the card back home, wrapped it in its blanket, put it away again, and went to sleep hungry but happy that he'd done the right thing. Maybe it was when he lived in the other car, the one before he got his Chevy. Was that car green?

Harold did not celebrate Hallowe'en, though he liked to watch it. On this particular fall afternoon, he was looking forward to more burning tires tonight, and pumpkins thrown from truck windows. Maybe some candy or popcorn too if he went to Snooky's backdoor. He was also feeling very self-satisfied, having been given the role of Joseph in the Christmas pageant. And while it was not a speaking part (of course Harold had never had a speaking part), it did carry some weight and it was certainly better than his last year's role as The Camel Driver, Harold Mosby. But right now it was a long time till candy and popcorn, and Harold was hungry. He figured if he just happened to show up at Snooky's kitchen door around now, he'd be given a little supper. Just to tide him over.

The shortcut from Harold's to the Rectory was through the dump. Harold didn't like the dump at any time of day, especially not at nearly dark, because he knew the rats were there looking for food, too. Harold hated the rats. Some of them were huge, and they all had lots of teeth. But it was getting late and dark, and if he did not want to miss supper, he figured he had no choice.

He went through the little stand of trees and crawled over the sagging fence around the dump. He was just about to make a run for it across the muddy, tire-tracked ground, past the big Mercedes and to safety from the rats, when, in the fading light, he saw a figure hunched over on the ground. Harold stopped short and held his breath. It looked like Buzz, and Buzz looked like he was praying. Maybe he was practicing his part in the manger scene? But it looked like Buzz was holding hands with the dirt.

Harold came a little closer. Did he want Buzz to see him? Should he, Harold, slip sideways into the twilight and take the long-cut to Snooky's? Not that Buzz seemed to be noticing him. Actually, Buzz looked very sad. He crouched, still as he could be, with his hand in the dirt.

"I am Joseph," said Harold to himself, "And that means I can do some help." This was quite a new kind of thought for Harold to have. So (and of course Harold was curious, too) he crept closer to Buzz, and closer, and finally was standing right at his side, though Buzz had never once looked up.

Thinking hard, to his role in the play, Harold put his hand, in stately fashion (sort of like he'd seen Father Kildare do to the grocery store checkout lady, or to someone on Main Street during the Memorial Day parade prayer and dedication service) on Buzz's shoulder and remained silent. Minutes passed, and the day slid further towards the dusty orange sun, the rising fog, the heavy yellow moon on the horizon.

And, it was getting colder. And Harold was getting hungrier. He stood there, with his hand on Buzz's shoulder, but thought about pork chops, potatoes, meatloaf, chicken in an oven pan, and of pork chops, again. But, he also tried to do his new part. Stand here, he thought, and be an important bystander. Like Joseph.

At last the sun was down and it was dark and Buzz had not seemed to feel Harold's hand. Buzz had not looked up, and Harold had remained looking into the distance (his directions for the play: look off into the distance and don't move, not even your head,

Harold). But finally, his stomach got the better of his patience. The thought that Snooky might scrape the pork chop leftovers into the dog bowl on the floor and the dog would eat them, and Harold didn't want to take that chance. So he looked down at Buzz and squeezed at his shoulder, just a little. When Buzz slowly looked up at him, Harold saw thin clean stripes down his face. Buzz stared up at Harold just as though they hadn't gone to elementary school together. It scared Harold a little, but he remained firm in his role.

Buzz cleared his throat and said, "Harold? I've found, look at this. I think this is, aw, shit, I think this is, remember that girl used to live around here?" And Harold, thinking almost nothing but how hungry he was and of his part in the play, nodded, as slowly and carefully as he could without moving his head too much. "Well," Buzz went on, "then don't this look to you like her?" Again, Harold nodded. "Me, too. Shit," said Buzz, looking back at the purse, the bones, and at the cinders and dirt where, who knew how far down, was the rest of . . . and in what condition now. Buzz began to sob.

But Harold knew what to do. Get my friend to an inn, he thought. That's the next part of what to do. Doing what the director had told him at tryouts, he leaned over, grabbed Buzz gently under the armpits, and urged him up on his feet. He kept one arm around Buzz and with the other, he pointed in the distance to the lights of the town. Then he turned Buzz towards the lights, took his arm, and led him down the ancient wasteland of trash towards the Rectory and Snooky's marinated veal.

Chapter III

In which Nearly Everyone Gets the News
And Makes a Trip to the Dump

The stove had gone out. Fido woke up, opened her mouth wide, wider, and jumped off the couch. It was dark, it was cold. No lights were on, no supper cooking, no supper in her dish. Adele snored on. Fido jumped back onto the couch and put her forehead against Adele's chin and went "mowr" and shoved a little. With a start, Adele woke up. Where? What? And then she clumsily reached out to encompass Fido and pat her a bit. Heavens. I've slept the afternoon away and let the fire go out. She stiffly sat up, stiffly got up, stiffly pulled down her sweater, shivered. She felt around in the gloom for the table, for her glasses on the table. Found them on the sideboard. Went into the dark kitchen, turned on the overhead, squinted at the clock: 5:17, minus the three fast minutes. With Fido slithering around her ankles, Adele went into the woodshed, gathered up an armful of split birch.

Glancing out the woodshed door, she could see that the Store was busy, many trucks and cars parked out front, just about closing time. The street lights were on. The smell of nearly frozen pumpkin was—was—was slicing, yes, through the night air. Pranks again tonight? She wondered if Hallowe'en lasted three or four days everywhere in the world, or just here? What was tonight? Adele could see Snooky's kitchen windows all steamed up. Yes, supper, she thought. Will do us all good.

She came back into her kitchen, went through to the middle room, dropped the logs into the old woodbox. Lifted the lid of the stove, poked among the embers, adjusted the damper, dropped in some dry kindling. Without thinking, she wiped her hands on her hips, which, without thinking, she'd been doing for years. If she had ever caught herself doing it, she'd have thought: oh, just like Gram used to do. Made her skirts all dirty. I always used to wish she wouldn't do that.

Supper. Fido, first. Something else? The shop? Go back over and lock up? No, did that. Probably hadn't been many people to shop, anyhow. Oh well, we all deserve a nap now and then. Something, though. Trick or treaters! That was it! She'd bought two large bags of assorted Kraft caramels. Now, where had she put them? She checked the stove, saw it had caught, turned to look for the caramels. Someplace. Any minute now, there'll be a knock on the door. Better put on the porch light, too. But something kept pushing its way into her mind. No trick or treaters, but Glinda. Where was Glinda. Was the letter a joke from somebody, a total fake? If not, then where was she? Adele didn't know if she was more nervous that Glinda was coming, or that Glinda had not already arrived. So unlike her to be late.

Adele rummaged through the bread wrappers and folded scraps of tinfoil in the drawer next to the sink. She has been so thrifty all her life, so careful and safe, saving. There was something to be said for that. After all, bread wrappers were as good as plastic wrap to cover the little blue and red and yellow margarine cups she saved and filled with half a cup of leftover soup, a bit of corned beef and beets, a spoon or two of pudding. And why should she throw away that last little end of tinfoil that always seemed to be left on the roll, just when you thought there was enough to cover the rhubarb crisp, but there wasn't? Those little ends were good for reheating half a baked potato, or a couple of fish sticks. It didn't seem right to waste. Now take Glinda—she would never even use a lipstick more than four or five times, let alone save bread wrappers. Adele sniffed. It was Glinda, single-handed, that was ruining the planet, she joked to herself. No caramels among the bread wrappers; the drawer got stuck and she hurt her knee against it.

Usually, privately poking fun at Glinda made her feel better, but tonight it didn't seem to help. Where could the caramels be? The goblins and skeletons and Martians would be here any minute.

And there she was, empty-handed, and then they'd pour Mazola oil on her front steps so she would slip and fall, or else they'd soap the windows of the shop with swears. Adele went into the cold guest room off the kitchen. There was just a chance she'd gone in there to shoo Fido off the bedspread and had been carrying the caramels with her at the time. Sure enough, there they were, side by side on the dresser.

The room was deathly cold. She hated this room. If it were possible, she'd have it hacked off the rest of the house. But it was a pretty room, and though sometimes Gram had done her sewing in here, it had always been kept ready in case a guest should come. Adele thought she remembered a distant cousin, one summer, maybe two cousins. Could recall the bend of her grandmother's neck while she sat in a rocker in a good light, mending sheets and elbows. Not unpleasant memories, Adele thought; so why did she hate this room so much?

Glinda had always been after Gram to let her move into it. "I hate having to share a room, especially with poky old Adele," Glinda had whined. "I hate it! I hate, it! Let me have this pwetty room, Gwammy, pweeze? pweeze?" But Gram, for once, stayed firm. No, this was for guests. Glinda's room with Adele was perfectly good enough for two young girls, just growing up. So Glinda had taken to trashing the guest room, defiling it a little, messing things up, leaving her stuff in there, or taking a nap on the bed when no one was home and leaving the spread rumpled, things like that. Naps with her shoes on.

One summer Sunday, ages ago, maybe all of them were still in high school. Anyway, Buzz was invited for Sunday dinner. Gramps was still alive. Buzz was doing the yardwork that summer, and cut their grass. A mercy he didn't run over his own foot, he was so smitten with Glinda by then. She was sunbathing that year, on a little patch of grass behind the woodshed. She treated Buzz like a servant, and refused to speak or open her eyes when he carefully mowed around her blanket. Then, as though the rattle of the push-mower were an affront to her sensibilities, she would suddenly rise, scoop up her magazines, baby oil, pillow, blanket, yank up her swimsuit, and stalk into the house. Flushed, clumsy, Buzz would accidentally run the mower into Gram's zinnia bed.

Adele couldn't now remember who had invited him to dinner that Sunday. She was cooking a roast and boiling some potatoes. The table was set for five and Buzz was about to arrive. There was lemonade. Glinda rushed into the kitchen, looking wild, and said "So where's my yellow sweater?" Adele, stirring a pot, didn't look up. "What yellow sweater?" "You know what sweater! I left it right there on the bed." "You know you're not supposed to put things on that bed. Gram doesn't like it." "Fat cow! You fat cow! You put my sweater someplace. Where is it? You tell me this minute," and Glinda began to pinch Adele's red arm above the elbow. "Fat cow, you tell me where you put the sweater or you'll be so sorry I can't tell you." Adele stared into the boiling potatoes, as though she hadn't heard a word.

Glinda ran into the guest room and there was a crashing of glass, the thud of pillows hitting the wall, wooden chairs hitting the floor. Adele dropped her spoon and ran into the room.

"I told you you'd be sorry, fat cow," Glinda screamed. "Take that. And that," and the rest of the milk-glass dresser set hit the wallpaper.

"O Glinda, please please don't. Please don't," and Adele almost cried again remembering it, remembering how Gram would feel when she saw. "Oh, please don't."

"And now I'm leaving and you'll be lucky if I ever come back," shrieked Glinda, pulling the white bedspread onto the floor and stomping on it. "Good-*bye*."

"You can't leave! Buzz is coming! Dinner's all ready! You know he's coming! He'll be here any minute! Please don't spoil things, please Glinda. I'll help you clean this up later. We'll just shut the door now and figure out what to do later."

"Do, schmoo, Buzz, scuzz, big deal, Cow Face, you figure it out," and Glinda had run out the door, jumped into a car which had evidently been waiting the whole time, and the boy—whoever it was driving—peeled out of the driveway in a storm of gravel and dust. Adele put her hand against her heart (another thing she'd unconsciously do the rest of her life) and leaned against the doorjamb. Just then Gram and Gramps came home from church with Buzz trailing behind them. Nothing to do but close the door to the guest room and try to think later how to clean it up and keep it from Gram. Maybe Adele would be able to find another milk-glass dresser set for sale, someplace. She pulled the door softly behind her and went back to the kitchen.

For a while, she and Buzz and Gram and Gramps sat in the parlor waiting for Glinda. The ice melted in the tall glasses on the dining room table. They talked about the weather, and church that morning, and the sermon, and the heat. Finally Buzz had said, "Something smells awful good, Del." (He was the only person who had ever called her that.) And she had said, "Glinda must be held up some place," and Buzz had nodded and helped Gram into the dining room.

Adele got some new ice. Gramps carved the shrunken roast. They sat down, Gram said grace, and they ate in silence. All this had been a long time ago. Buzz helped Adele with the dishes. Gram went to take a nap; Gramps went to listen to the radio. Buzz and Adele stacked the clean plates in the cupboard, wiped the crumbs off the table, straightened the chairs, and pulled down the blinds. Then they had walked down to the Variety Store (gone now) in the hot, fading afternoon. Buzz bought her a Moxie, and then they had walked up the hill to the cemetery and visited Buzz's dead relatives for a while. They sat on a fallen headstone for a long time, not talking, under a half-moon, with crickets in the uncut grass, and a whippoorwill calling in the dusk. Without doing anything obvious, or talking much, they managed to comfort each other.

Adele heard the jangle of the doorbell and came to herself with a jump. Hallowe'en had begun in earnest. She gathered up the bags of caramels and shut the guest room door behind her as she hurried to greet the first batch of little beggars.

Snooky took a sip of cooking sherry, wiped his hands, and squeezed the veal in the pan. He burned his fingers, as per usual.

He couldn't recall for the life of him where he'd read that a really excellent cook could tell if meat was perfectly done by squeezing it, or was it pressing it? He was sure Julia hadn't said it, as Julia would never suggest the cook do anything painful, so maybe he had read it someplace. Laugh, laugh, and who had time to read? Could it have been in *The New Yorker*? And when could he have read *The New Yorker*? Up here, what would be the point? And who would write about squeezing meat in *The New Yorker*, anyhow? And how was the meat supposed to feel? Softer? Harder? Meatier? Snooky ran his thumb and forefinger under the cold tap, rolled his eyes to the ceiling, went back to the pan, and pressed down on the top of the veal cutlets with a wooden spoon. Mainly, he smelled the sizzling meat and licked a smear of Marsala from the spoon and felt very hungry, considering it was such an uncivilized hour to eat.

Little spaetzle bubbled in one pot. The veal hissed in another. Time for the peas? The package said "petit pois," and they cost a bloody mint, but the peas looked suspiciously gross as they rattled, zap-frozen, one at a time into a third pot with a walnut of butter plus one teas. of water. "They'll say *anything*; 'petit' my buns," said Snooky to himself, out loud, glancing at Pussums and then at the wall clock. An unheard-of hour, an hour for old folks, for field peasants, a wretched uncivilized habit, eating at 5:30. But the Padre went to bed around eight, and was lucky to stay alive that long. Personally, Snooky thought eight was the civilized time to eat, and around midnight a civilized time to go to bed. Though up here in the hills, as Snooky often remarked to nearly anyone, even the street lamps went to bed with the birds. Then he would always add, as he passed or poured something, "That's one of my sitting-down jokes!" and everyone always laughed.

But once Snooky had done their trays, eaten, and watched the news; gotten Padre cleaned up and settled down for the night; straightened the kitchen and set the pans to soak; settled things to marinate, thaw, or mold for tomorrow; let Pussums out, then back in; watered his pots of windowsill parsley and thyme; checked on the Padre; had his own warm bath at last and a little read of Julia in bed, an early night of it did not seem too decadent, not this once, considering what he had been through today.

Five twenty-five! At 5:30 sharp, not a second later, that supper tray had to go through that swinging door. A minute later, Snooky swore to Adele quite often, a second later, and that Godforsaken walker would go thump, thump, thump in the same Godforsaken spot on the carpet of the parlor, wonder the rug wasn't in positive shreds, whereupon Pussums would set up a ghastly howl, and Snooky wouldn't even be able to think, much less cook, over the racket. "Slave driver," Snooky said. "Monster. Wind-bag. Tyrant. Old has-been."

And "Farmers. Hicks. Peasants," he added, as he stirred, pressed, sipped, licked, pinched, and bustled and brooded. At the "ding" of the timer he drained the spaetzle, drained the peas, dumped both onto warmed plates. Flipped the veal, turned it low, added another "splash," as Julia called it, of Marsala, slightly re-filled his jelly glass with another nip of cooking sherry, and reached for the two supper trays. "Riffraff. Who but riffraff would eat at this ungodly hour and get us into this ungodly rush?" he asked Pussums.

Tap-tap. Tap-tap. "Not, oh Lord, already?" said Snooky. "Slave driver." But the tap-tap was soft, not the imperious thump of the walker being pounded in one place. And the tap-tap was at the kitchen door, not coming from the front parlor.

"And *now* what, at this hour, don't they realize it's . . . COMING!" he added, shoving his jelly glass behind the Christmas cactus, stabbing off the flame under the veal, fluffing up his sideburns, and heading for the door. Then he thought "Oh, naturally, Hallowe'en! And the peasants' monstrous greedy offspring already, not even dark!" (Though it was.) He reached for the big wooden bowl he'd spent the afternoon filling and arranging: colored pop-corn balls, wrapped in waxed paper. Mars bars, small ones, good for little fingers. Polished red McIntosh. Small bags of dry-roasted peanuts. Foil-wrapped chocolate coins. Marshmallow pumpkins with smiles. Bags of candy corn. "God," thought Snooky, "they'll eat anything," and had counted several times to make sure he had enough.

He took up the big bowl, flicked on the porch light, expecting at least two Ninja turtles, a couple of ghouls, one Barney, a Mickey Mouse, a ballerina. He anticipated their small piping voices, their extended plastic pumpkins, their little held-up hands, their grateful "thank-you's" on the night air. He opened the door, holding the bowl behind his back.

But instead of turtles or ballerinas, he looked into the faces of Buzz and Harold, so distressed, so gray and distressed that, for once, Snooky hardly had time to pretend to recoil from surprise or to mime what nuisance could this be now. One word came to his mind, by way of his neighborly eye: trouble. There's some kind of trouble. But aloud he said, "Boys! In costume so early! Oh, do come in! Oh no, not busy at all!"

Harold and Buzz waited on the bottom step, looking at each other, waiting for each other to go first, so Snooky had to say, "*Really. Would* you mind?" while holding the door wider open. (There's one veal Marsala ruined, he thought. But he also thought: they need me. Somehow they need me. Something has happened.) Without thinking, he pushed the wooden bowl of popcorn balls, Mars bars, and apples in front of them. Both looked in, hesitated, looked up, looked at each other, and shook their heads. Harold licked his teeth, but his tongue looked dry. Buzz was, Snooky told Adele later that night, "positively pea green, my dear, green as a pea!"

Snooky said, "Oh do sit down, let me fix the Parson's tray, you know how he is if he has to wait five seconds! A little chop! A sprinkle of peas! There we go! A dumpling or two for the Old Dumpling! Perfect! And a nappie right there! And . . . rush . . . it . . . into him. And, . . ." (Thump, thump, thump began) "And, be back in two sec's and will find a treat for *you*!" He kicked open the swing door with one foot, picked up the tray, flung on some silver, and padded down the dark hall, crowing "Coming! Coming! Din-din!" Pussums growled at the two men, showed his tiny teeth, and went back to his basket. Buzz and Harold did not look at each other. They waited, still standing, needing to be asked twice to sit down.

"VEAL!" they could hear from upfront in the house, "Veal, veal, veal! Yes, fit to eat! Let me cut it *up* for you! Get your fingers *out* of that!" Silence. Buzz and Harold waited, looked at the floor. "This *is* the sodding channel you always watch. Always *watch*! Watch! Yes, that *is* your weather girl!" And footsteps, slams, footsteps, and Snooky flew back through the swinging door.

"You have no idea," he began, but then remembered his audience and the air of something more than trick or treating or begging a supper they had brought in with them from the darkness. "I think," he said, "I see two boys before me who could use a little something," and he reached into the cupboard for the good bourbon, his eyebrows raised a little in mock question, which Harold and Buzz answered by nodding with mock regret, but implicit "guess we don't mind." Snooky took down two good glasses and poured an inch in each, set the glasses on the table, motioned the men to sit down. They did. Harold held onto Buzz's sleeve with one filthy clawlike hand. But Buzz didn't seem to notice.

"Well," said Snooky, "what a day!" He paused. Harold fiddled with his glass, then took a big slurpy drink and wiped his chin on his sleeve. Buzz just sat there. Harold looked at Buzz. Buzz looked into space. Harold looked at Snooky. Snooky looked at them both.

"Seems to me, boys, something is de-finitely up?" Harold nodded. Buzz looked sick. "Buzz?" said Snooky, There was no point asking Harold, though he could tell from Harold's eyes that there was something Buzz had to tell. "Buzz?" Snooky poured a little more bourbon in both glasses, and poured a little into his jelly glass. Starch, he thought. Dutch courage. Courage, anyhow.

Buzz looked up. "Dump," he said. "Found, dump, pocketbook, things, her, dead." Harold nodded and nodded and did not let go of Buzz's dirty sleeve. "Dead. Pocketbook, things, ring, her, dump, you know," said Buzz.

"Fabulous," thought Snooky, and "good-bye veal chop, farewell bubble bath." Aloud he said, "Tell me again? Buzz? more slowly?"

Harold nodded. Buzz said, "In the dump. Body. Her. Dead."

"Right," said Snooky. "Right. Now, let's try again. You have a body in the dump, dead? Buzz, it's Hallowe'en! Remember? Forget? It's the kids, the hideous teenagers, they are pretending to be something, dead and so forth." It made Snooky a little miserable when he heard himself getting loud and simple, over-clear. They can understand a normal voice, he reminded himself. They really can. "Look, Buzz, it's just the kids. You know, they're putting on an act tonight, probably trying to scare you, you know? Look. Have another drink, and let me see if I can rustle up a little snack of something."

Harold nodded vigorously, but then looked at Buzz, and seeing that Buzz shook his head, once, Harold shook his head once, too. But Snooky pretended not to see this, got up, took two plates from the cupboard, put them on the table, two napkins, two knives, two forks, (buy a little time here, he thought) and carefully placed the last two chops on the plates, gave each a little stack of peas, divided up the dumplings, cast an eye on the clock—5:50—and plugged in the electric kettle. "Oh let the Old Holy get involved in the weather for once, please God," he thought, as he licked his fingers and looked with regret into the now empty pots.

He put a plate, the silver, a napkin in front of each man. He sat down. "So, there's someone dead. In the dump. Right?" Buzz sat there. Harold ate. "Pretending to be dead, right?"

Buzz sat there. "No," he said at last. "Dead, really dead. Really her. I found her. Really dead. Bones. She's nothing but bones."

And to think, thought Snooky, I could be in San Francisco right now. The trolley cars. The views. The delicious little evenings. The talk. The art. Wearing my clothes, my good clothes. All so tony.

"Who's bones, Buzz?" Snooky leaned across the table. "Who is bones?"

"Her. Bones. Ring. I know her ring and it's her ring. I know that ring all right."

Harold nodded, even violently. Snooky thought. Should he call Adele, ask if she could pop over for a minute? Then suddenly, but softly, he brought both plump hands, palms down, onto the kitchen table. "Boys. This calls for a better judgment than mine," and he got up, pulling the plug on the electric kettle as he passed it, and went out through the swing door again.

A few minutes went by. Buzz and Harold could hear a rising

and falling murmur through the walls. They both ate. Harold wet his finger and ran it around his plate. Buzz pushed a pea until it fell onto the floor, and Pussums, with a snarl, grabbed it up. Snooky returned, sat down, looked them both in the eye. "He says," he said, "Police. The only thing to do. If you're certain, then we must call the Police. There are some Police, aren't there?"

Buzz, his mouth full, looked up and nodded. Harold ran a black finger around his empty plate and nodded, licked his finger and ran it round the plate again. So much for veal chops, thought Snooky. Is any cause a good cause around this place? "So. Yes. Police. Now, how do we call the Police?"

"On the phone," said Buzz, "it's on the phone." And Snooky lifted the receiver and saw the sticker between the two little knobs—sure enough, "For Emergency Assistance Dial 911" it said; and he did, and waited.

"You are on hold," said a voice, "just hold on." The line seemed to go dead. Snooky could feel himself sweating. Right then there was a weak knock at the back door. Snooky mimed to Harold to get the bowl, go to the door, open the door, hold out the bowl. Harold understood, and he did all that, checking each step with Snooky who was still holding the phone against his ear and nodding, and waving his hand. Harold opened the door to a bat, a very short cowboy, and a pirate. "Trick or . . ." they began. But when they looked up and saw Harold standing over them with the huge bowl, the three gave a high yelp and scrabbled down the steps, screaming and running. The bat dropped his bag. Harold looked out into the empty darkness, leaned down and picked up the little bag, placed it in the bowl, and closed the door. He sat down, holding the bowl in his lap, looking puzzled and sadder.

"Gotcha," said a deep voice on the other end of the line, "Rescue."

"We need help up here!" said Snooky, "are you the Police? We need you right now, at once, please."

"Naw, this is Rescue. Who is this?"

"This is 'The Rectory,' thank you very kindly, and we need to speak to the Police. Are you Police?"

"Naw, I tode-ja, Rescue. Snooky? Is that you? This is Gerald here, down to the fire house, what's up up there?"

"Oh, heavens," said Snooky. "Look. We need the Police. I'm just too overwhelmed with people and problems here, I can't tell you, Gerald, I'm so glad it's you, would you call the Police for me and tell them to hurry? Buzz and Harold are here and there's a body or something."

"Gotcha," said Gerald. Thinking, so the old preacher popped off at last, did he? "Just settle down there, Snooky, we'll be right up and I'll get the police too, if you think it's really necessary. Under the circumstances, I mean. It's Hallowe'en, you know, they're pretty goddamned busy, but I'll try. Meantime, I'll give the boys a ring; we'll suit up, and get right up there."

"It was Gerald," said Snooky, hanging up. "They're coming." He sat down in his chair. He wiped his forehead with his apron. What was the point of trying to get more information from these two? And he probably ought not to give them any more whiskey, either. And he probably ought not to have any more himself. The clock ticked, and the distant sound of a commercial came from the front of the house. Snooky reached into the big bowl in Harold's lap, fished around, took out a small Mars bar, made a face, un-wrapped it, and ate it.

Puck Diddles got the news first. He was sitting in his car, a chocolate colored Caddy, which had a vanity plate, BRNSGR. (Not that Puck really needed a vanity plate, he told himself. Everyone knew him. And his car.) He was working on his gums with a wooden match and reading today's paper by the light of his dash-board. He turned to the obituaries, ran his eye down the list of names. Had the owner of the pink Lincoln died? Anyone whose relative would need some home improvement before they could sell off the property?

It was Puck's custom to read the obituaries in the three most local dailies, and pick out those recently departed who had held property, and upon their deliverance to the Almighty, to pay a call as soon as tasteful to their distraught and grieving relatives and offer to ease their burdens by siding "at a very fair price" the departed's real estate holdings. "Vinyl," Puck would murmur, "is the only modern way to go this day and age. Lasts forever. Looks good, any kind of weather, it'll hold up, no more problems for you and yours. You've got more than enough on your plate right now, and the sale value of your granny's house? It'll skyrocket, once we get that siding on there. Now I don't want to bother you at a time like this, but my company is prepared to offer you add-a-rooms, metal awnings, garages, just about anything you might be needing. Now look, you and your family think it over, and I'll give you a ring—estimate, free—in a day or so. When did you say the . . . well, when you're ready, all right? Call you tomorrow. Such a shock. So sorry to hear about it."

Though he was no longer a selectman, Puck still considered himself a sort of behind-the-scenes "overseer of the poor." That, or someone "dedicated to helping Maine's economy," keeping life the way it ought to be. Not too many folks into siding, though. Preferred clapboards, rot and all, no matter how much evidence he showed them in regards to vinyl's superiority to wood and paint. Backwards, he thought. Just won't enter the twentieth century, that's all. (He didn't know that it had been suggested, more than once, and by different people, too, that his vanity plate should actually read SLMLRD.)

Puck had a police scanner in BRNSGR. This was a tax write-off, or at least he made it one by buying a newer and bigger one each year and charging it to the national debt by saying he "needed it for his estate business." Puck spent a lot of time in his car, sitting there, reading the papers, dreaming, eyeing properties, combing his hair in the mirror, listening to his scanner, waiting for any reports of car accidents or lovers' quarrels that had led to crimes of passion. He got some good leads this way. People in shock would be glad for his help, and funerals were expensive, and old run-down, peeling houses hard to sell, and Puck reasoned he was there when folks needed him. He often said this to his dates. "You know," he'd say, "people don't really understand the home improvement business. They think you're in it for yourself, well, they just couldn't be more wrong. In its way, it's community service, you know? Know what I mean? How's your steak, sweetie, tender enough?"

Puck started doodling on his mini legal pad. He was considering making an offer on that pink Lincoln that he figured would be coming up for sale, real soon. In addition to listening to the scanner and reading obits, Puck also had a buddy who drove the Meals on Wheels wagon. He heard, from this buddy, that, probably within a week or so, the pink Lincoln would be ownerless. If he got it, Puck had pretty much decided to get a second vanity plate—CTNCND.

The scanner crackled and blinked in the darkness. Puck heard a gargle, indicating someone was on the air. He looked out the car window. Leaves were blowing, a good sign. Well, a bad sign, of course. Probably someone had skidded on the slimy road. Could be serious business. Puck turned up the volume.

"There's a call from the Rectory or whatever the hell they call it," Gerald's voice came across. "Got a body. Wanna check it out? Think we'd better."

"Gotcha. You sure you got it right? The old preacher die in his tray or sumpin'?"

"Well, seems like he would, but no, that ain't it, evidently. Just talked to 'em again, they say there's a body found up to the dump. Couple of witnesses. They're at the Rectory right now."

"OK. I'll swing by and get 'em. Call for back-up and tell 'em to meet me at the dump, OK?"

"OK. Gotcha. Over and out."

Puck did not wait to hear the call for back-up. He slammed BRNSGR into gear and headed for the Library.

He was not, of course, the only citizen of Bosky Dells to have a scanner. About half the town owned at least one, and on a night like Hallowe'en, most of them were on. In fact, most ran 24 hours a day, 7 days a week, 365 days a year.

Within five minutes of Gerald's call to other Rescue members, there was a long line of cars heading to the dump. Those who did not have a car rode their riding lawn mowers or ATV's. Others hollered and hitched a ride, their mouths full of supper, in the bed of a neighbor's pick-up. A real honest-to-God body at the dump? Not just somebody horsing around? Could be an unidentified murder victim. Maybe a spot on *Unsolved Mysteries,* one of everybody's favorite programs, next to *America's Funniest Home Videos* and *Wheel of Fortune.* (Puck lusted, really lusted, and not in his heart, either, for Vanna White.)

Wilma Look, the librarian, did not resemble Vanna White at all; nevertheless, since his divorce, she and Puck had been keeping company for years. She was at the Library tonight, it being written in her contract that the librarian would be present at the Library on Hallowe'en night, no matter which day of the week. This thoughtful stipulation served three purposes. One, the Library was in a central location and all the kids could walk there, assuring everyone at least one treat. Second, the bathroom was nice, and mothers appreciated that. Third, lights and a live presence in the building deterred the merrymakers from spraying shaving cream on the stained-glass windows with the names of Homer, Longfellow, Plato, Emerson, or from covering the bust of Shakespeare (or was it Lamb?) with contraceptive foam and leaving the disgusting can behind, as they had done one year.

Wilma heard a knocking on the door, which she had not yet unlocked. I'm going to have my sandwich first, she thought. They can just come back later. But the knocking was so insistent and loud that she folded up her sandwich, slammed it back in her brown bag, and got up to open the door, one hand on a hip. "Heavens," she began, when she saw it was Puck.

"Come on, Wilma, lock up," he said, puffing. "Let's go. There's a body at the dump."

"A body? Are you kidding? A dead body?"

"Of course it's a dead body. Why would a live body be at the dump? Come on, grab your coat and lock up."

"Well, I'm not supposed to, you know. I'm supposed to be here all evening. I don't know."

"I'm giving you three seconds, okay? You wanna come or not? I can certainly find my way there without you, I just thought you'd like to come along."

"Well, I would. I'm just not supposed to. Oh, I guess it wouldn't matter for a few minutes. Will we be gone long?"

"How do I know how long? For Pete's sake, Wilma, if you want to come, come. If not, not. I did this for a favor, you know,"

"Now, Puck, I know that. Please don't raise your voice. Just come inside for a minute, let me check things, get my coat, okay? No need to raise your voice."

(Would Vanna White need to "check things?" Jesus, probably not. Vanna'd just say, "Take me to it, Puck," and away we'd go. Fuss, fuss, fuss. Women.)

Wilma put on her gray coat. She went down to the basement to make sure the cellar door was locked. She came back up the stairs. Looked at her watch. Turned down the thermostat. Wrote out a notice: Be Right Back. Taped it to the glass of the front door. Turned off the lights in the Children's Reading Room. Picked up the phone for some reason, though it had not rung. Hung it up. Checked her pockets. Smiled at Puck. Rolled down the top of her lunch bag, tight. Pulled out her scarf.

"Now or never," said Puck. "I'm leaving. Do what you want," and he went out the door and down the steps to his car, Wilma tripping after him, pulling on her gloves.

By the time they got to the dump, parking was tight. They had to walk almost a quarter of a mile before they got close enough to hear or see what was happening. Even at a distance though, the sight was spectacular. More like Fourth of July.

Red and blue cruiser lights flashed like space-war fireflies. For whatever reason, since no automobiles were involved, nevertheless a couple of wrecker service tow trucks were flashing orange and yellow. Someone had built a bonfire and the sacred-oil-factory folks were feeding it old chairs and wooden crates and bags of dried leaves and landfill wood the power company had discarded as too punky to burn. Buzz was maneuvering Earth Angel, his backhoe, into place to dig another scoop away from a low mound. The body?

All around the scene, in a circle, stood the village children, their faces glowing fluorescent red and orange, green and magenta, in the flickering flames. Adults stood behind them. Slowly, methodically, the children fed candy from their bags into their gaping pink mouths. Snow White picked her nose. A Ninja Turtle scratched his green bottom intently. Two Draculas kicked a can back and forth between them. A Mickey Mouse cried against his mother's knees. All of a sudden, a hush fell over the whole crowd. Puck pushed Wilma ahead of him, and he tried to see over the heads, all bending forward in one motion. Wilma tugged at his coat.

"Puck, what is it? Can you tell? What's happening? Is it somebody we know?" But Puck didn't reply. A gust of wind came up and the trees rattled in the heavy silence, a silence broken only by the snap of the fire and the ragged humming of Earth Angel's idling motor. The air smelled mucky, stale, hoary, smoky. The moon rose.

Carefully (for a backhoe) the bones were unearthed, and lay spread beneath the various glares. The crowd gasped. Someone screamed, but it was a little theatrical, for effect only. The pile of bones, with six or seven policemen helping, was gingerly moved to a white stretcher on the ground. The hand with the ring bobbed up and down as the stretcher was lifted into the back of an ambulance. Among the children standing close, a white rabbit with pink ears waved back.

"Okay, folks," said a loudspeaker, "let's all go home quietly now. It's all over now. Let's just all go home." No one moved.

Harold crouched in the shadows, his head buried in his arms. His body shook with sobs. A couple of rats watched him. He'd never seen anyone dead before. What was this all about? Was it his fault? Raising his dirty face, with white smudges on it, he looked at the sky and thought it was strange that there were so many hard stars and that none of them was twinkling.

It wasn't ten o'clock yet, but Adele had been in bed for hours with an aspirin, first; and then her rubber earplugs in place, so hadn't heard a thing going on (as she told the police the next day) since around eight o'clock or thereabouts. Her doorbell had started ringing just about suppertime, and when she ran out of caramels, she'd turned the porch light off. Later, she was able to tell the police she'd run out of caramels at almost exactly 6:00, no matter what her kitchen clock said, because the carillon (on tape) from the loudspeaker of the bell tower of the church had clicked on, played "Abide With Me," followed by fifteen minutes of well-beloved hymns. The police checked, and determined that "Abide With Me" was, in fact, the first song on the tape.

Strange, thought Adele, letting Fido out and hearing the old hymn grind loud, slow, tinkly, and off-key over the night scene of freshly-lit tires, new toilet paper in the elm, an outhouse—moved for a joke onto the porch of the Store. Large adult men, screaming with laughter, curses, and robust challenges, jumped back and forth through the roiling flames in the street, emptying cans of kerosene or beer onto the burning tires. Some of their girlfriends, or "women" as Adele called them, dressed in tight jeans and tight jean jackets and with identical perms, leaned against one dark car, smoking, drinking beer from bottles, and discussing a baby shower they were planning. What games? "That's a real fun game," said one of them; "Jesus, I love that game." A mother herded a princess and a frog up the street, making a wide cut around the leaping men, and yelling, "You little shits, do I have to tell you again to get the hell over here away from them?"

Shaking her head at what the world had come to, and holding Fido safe in her arms, Adele came back into her house, turned off the porch light, pulled the green shades in her kitchen, and prayed they'd leave her alone. Alone is what she had to be. To think. What if Glinda really is coming back after she had promised and sworn and double-sworn never to set foot in town again. Because once, twenty-five, twenty-six, longer maybe, years ago, Adele had trusted Glinda because she could tell, for once, that Glinda was really really scared. "Swear to me Glinda," she had hissed, and Glinda had sworn and crossed her heart and rolled her eyes and sobbed and promised. Crossed her heart. Not much there to swear on, Adele remembered thinking at the time. But she had trusted Glinda because she had to trust her. She had no choice.

Adele fussed around her kitchen, listened to the raucous sounds from across the street, expected to hear sirens any minute. She sat down to her sardines and toast, her final cup of tea. Too worked up to eat, she thought, opening a can of baked beans and eating them cold. Just like Girl Scout outings, she thought for a pleasant second. But that recalled Glinda crossing her black heart and whispering, "Scout's honor, Adele, I swear."

I'll think about it tomorrow, thought Adele, and smiled because this was her favorite expression from one of her favorite books, and it seemed to fit so many situations. She put her cup, spoon, and plate into the sink, rinsed out the two cans, turned down the stove damper, turned out the lights, and climbed the dark stairs. Bath, book, earplugs, bed. Got to think. Got to be alone. Was Glinda really coming back, despite all her promises? In which case, where was she? And most of all, what did she want after all this time?

Got to get to Adele, thought Snooky, got to get to Adele before one of these clowns or busybodies gets there first. I've got to be there when Adele gets told. I've got to tell her.

He stood out of the smoke. The wind on the dump hill blew the bonfire higher and hotter and scudded the clouds across the moon and fanned the voices around the circle.

Who? It's that Glinda True, remember her? Left town about, I don't know, couple years ago, maybe? Naw, twenty or more, at least! Glinda True? It's Glinda. Glinda who? Someone you prolly don't recall, you just moved here. Who? Somebody we all knew. Yea, knew pretty good too, huh? Who is it? Do they know who it is? Yep, sure do. Found positive identi-fi-ca-shun. No doubt at all, they said. Who said? Who did you say it was? That Glinder, re-member Adele's cousin Glinder? She was in your class, weren't she? Oh, Glinder? That's her? How do they know? (No, Michelle, it isn't anything. Just a game, honey. Just a joke.) How do they know? Who are they talking about? I dunno—somebody lived here long time ago; let's go home. Who did it? Jeez, what a town. You can say that again. (Michelle, stop it honey. It's just a joke, stop it.)

Got to go, got to go, got to tell her, and Snooky slipped away from the lights and headed downhill in the darkness to Adele's.

There wasn't a light on at Adele's when he got there, not even upstairs, and the door was locked. Good; at least I got here first. Snooky knocked hard. Waited. Knocked. Thought of the bell. Pushed the bell and knocked at the same time. Leaned over and knocked on the window and rang the bell and kicked the door. Everything seemed quite clear but slowed down.

A little crack of light showed first, upstairs. The glow of inner light, the bulb on the stairs. Then he could hear the slush-slush of her slippers, then a crack of light in the kitchen, and then the door opened a little and Adele, her hair on end and one hand clutching a plaid flannel robe together under her chin, looked out.

"Glinda? Snooky! What in the world?"

"Adele, are you alone?" asked Snooky, looking into the kitchen.

He knows! thought Adele. He knows she's supposed to be here by now. How?

"Of course I'm alone, what did you think, who would anyhow? be here?" and Adele opened the door and Snooky came in. Unable to stop shaking and shivering, Adele pulled out a kitchen chair and sat down.

"Sit down, Adele, I've got something to tell you," said Snooky. He rubbed his small hands together and held them over the unlit burner of the gas stove. "Adele, prepare yourself for awful news. I came as fast as I could. How are you feeling?"

"Ready, I think," said Adele. His supper got burnt. Pussums was kidnapped by Hallowe'eners. Father Kildare fell out of his chair. Snooky is leaving for San Francisco at last. Glinda went to the Rectory first and confessed everything and the state police are already on their way and will be here soon and I've run out of caramels. No, that's not why they'd be coming. "Snooky, please, *you* sit down and tell me, what?"

"Your dear cousin is," said Snooky, "Glinda is, Adele, I'm so sorry. I'll do anything I can, believe me. Can I make you some tea? Get you a wee one? Don't fret about a thing, I'll do it all, I'll see you through this, I promise. Life! I can hardly bear it somedays, but I can bear this better than you, and I don't want you to worry about a thing, not the reception for after the funeral or a thing, promise? Oh Adele, at moments like this our friends are what count and that's why I rushed to be here first. These clods, gossips, morons, unsimpatico boors, had they gotten here ahead of me! Thank God, so really, I'm so glad. . . . ."

"Glinda," Adele interrupted, "is what? Please finish, dear Snooky, please do finish."

"Gone," Snooky said. "Passed away. Deceased. Well, dead, actually. Actually, I'd say quite dead. Oh, dear." And he broke into a flood of tears, and sat down. "Oh, I'm so glad to be here for you," and he held his little face in his hands and sobbed.

Adele reached into the napkin holder and handed him a wad of paper napkins. He blew his nose, and looked at Adele as if waiting for her to take charge.

"I just came from there," he continued, "came straight here. Of course. I was one of the first people at the dump, well I called the Police in the first place, and what I'm trying to say, Adele, though I'm sure I'm not doing too well at it, is that she was at the dump. She is dead, and she is at the dump."

If that isn't her all over, thought Adele. Keeps me waiting on pins and needles and goes to the dump first to jump in bed with Buzz, no doubt; no doubt can't go a minute without jumping in bed with someone. But wait, Buzz only works at the dump. Well, the truck then, the seat of the truck, no doubt. Glinda never was finicky about where, God knows. But could Buzz have stayed mad enough, heartbroken enough, after all these years, to . . . kill her?

"Did Buzz, did Buzz, was it Buzz?"

"Yes!" said Snooky, "of course Buzz did it. Buzz and Harold, but mainly Buzz and Earth Angel. Well, someone said he used just a spoon at first but when the spoon wasn't doing the job, he used a pitchfork, or they did, and then they told him to use Earth Angel, which seems a little brutal, but what else could he do? And the Police had given him permission, of course. They stood around and watched to make sure he did it right and didn't miss anything. I mean the ground is practically frozen, and a shovel would hardly have worked, though he did use a shovel at the end after Earth Angel had done the heavy part. Actually, I think, I hate to tell you this, Adele, but let's be strong. Actually I think I heard someone say they'd have to finish the job with dental picks. Just to make sure, you see. Though I can't pretend to understand that at all. I mean, she was really clean. Well, bare. I think they'll have to use chemicals now. Not that I understand these things. I mean, I hardly even watch crime shows! Well, the violence! So, I don't know the first thing about how this is done. But don't you think chemicals just to be sure?"

"Sure of what, exactly?" whispered Adele. I'm in shock, she thought. This is what it feels like. Why else would I think the state police were coming for Kraft caramels? Was Glinda this tough to kill? Was Buzz so angry all these years that he used the backhoe? It sounds like that, who was that, Russian priest they kept trying to kill, but he wouldn't die? They poisoned him, stabbed him, shot him, who was that? Well, she certainly must be dead.

"Sure that it's her, Adele! There's her purse full of identification and somebody said something about a ring on her, its, finger that she always evidently wore. But the bones, Darling, who could tell for sure without, you know, fancy tests with chemicals and things? I mean, bones all look alike, don't they?"

Adele felt ice-cold, then hot, then faint, then fainted. For the hundredth time today, Snooky had his hands full.

Chapter IV

In Which a Funeral Is Interrupted

By Monday morning, things had begun to calm down and get sorted out. The high-school "H.Y.C." (Help Your Community/work/study group) was sweeping up Main Street, shoveling pumpkins, toilet paper, beer cans, and tires into one big pile while their teacher, Dan, wet it all down with a long hose and rallied the lads to stay at it. The story of Saturday night had already required five free refills of coffee at the lunch counter. It is hard to say what the mood of the town was: busy, yet sobered; hung over, yet on the move; long faces, but with glittering eyes; quiet voices, yet rapid. Everyone had to go to the Store for a carton of molasses, or a single onion, or a can of evaporated milk, something like that. Already an envelope was scotch-taped to the edge of the cash register: "In Memory of Glinda True" penciled on it. Two state police sat in the cruiser parked next to the ice machine outside the Store, and occasionally one of them talked into a car phone. It drizzled a little. If looks could console, Adele received many consolations, as every glance on Main Street, at some time or other, went over to her still closed-up house. "She's taking it real well, real well," said one well-wisher who, in fact, had not seen Adele for weeks and hadn't noticed her then, but now wanted a part in the making of this morning's history.

The phones had been busy all of Sunday and today since dawn. The scanners had been on all night. Four women, the officers of the Ladies Auxiliary, were calling each other back and forth, trying to decide if a Benefit Supper was in order, and if so, who had the jello list, and how soon could they get things organized? One thought not, on the grounds that it wasn't actually like a death. But another wondered how else could they show Adele some community support? They couldn't come up with a satisfactory answer to this, so hung up to call other members.

The kids were back in school, but wan (up too late all weekend) and unruly (too excited; too much sugar) and the teachers, during their morning recess coffee break, discussed whether or not they should call in the district crisis counselor to help everybody talk through this. "Ventilate," one teacher kept saying. "These kids need support, and they need to ventilate their feelings." Seeing one little knot of second graders ventilating their feelings by burying a small girl in the grit of the playground—she was screaming—one boy was imitating a backhoe—the teachers went rushing out to intervene. "I told you," yelled the third-grade substitute. "We need to call in some professionals here! We need to get through this thing together!"

A CLOSED DUE TO DEATH IN IMM. FAMILY sign hung on the doorknob of About Thyme, thanks to Snooky who was trying to think of every little thing he could do. Happily, this early Monday morning, Father Kildare, tired from the news of the weekend, was still asleep. But Snooky, who had not slept at all for days (as he told Adele) stood at his kitchen window, stirring his cup of French Roast, and watching for signs of life to appear in Adele's kitchen window, or at least a puff of white smoke from her chimney. The green shades remained drawn, but as soon as Snooky saw white smoke, signifying that Adele had opened her dampers and stirred her fire, he reached for the phone.

"Hello," said Adele, not sounding like herself at all.

"Darling," said Snooky. "Adele, Dear Heart, are you up?"

Adele, who slept like a log, replied that she was, and that as soon as she made some coffee herself, would call him right back.

"Plans, darling," said Snooky. "We've just got to make some. There's the service, the flowers to think about. And who will do it? When will they let us have it? And a bite afterwards, here? your house? Adele, you must pull yourself together and let me do it all."

"Promise, Snooky, I'm all right, right as rain. I'll call you right back." And Adele hung up, wondering what she would wear today. What suited the occasion?

I'll wear the same thing I always wear, she said to herself. What's so special about today, after all? Just appear normal. But subdued. I'll wear my gray wool skirt and my tan sweater-coat. It's all over now. One day at a time. Keep it simple, stupid—which she'd read once on a bumper sticker and liked, and often reminded herself: keep it simple, stupid, and, I'll think about it tomorrow. She put the kettle on the stove; let Fido out the back door.

While she watched the kettle come to a boil, she thought: I could make a list of what I need to think about, and she looked around for paper. On the kitchen table next to the napkin holder and under a jar of mustard, was a folded piece of pink paper. Adele picked it up, fished for a pen in the jar of spoons, and then gave a horrible little scream. My God, the letter from Glinda. That was the hitch, wasn't it? Steady, old girl. Some Maxwell. Get dressed. One day at a time. The phone rang again.

"Hello. This is Adele. Yes, I have heard. Yes, awful shock. No, fine, really. Well, fine as I can be. A supper? It's very kind of you, but perhaps not . . . right . . . as of yet. Yes, she was. No, no one but Glinda and myself. No, not for quite some time. Yes, a good job, I believe. We're waiting to hear from the police. Perhaps no service at the church at all. I really haven't. . . . Thank you . . . yes, a cake would be lovely. No, chocolate would be fine. Thank you . . . thank . . . thank you for calling."

Before she could make her coffee, the phone rang again, then again, as it would for many days to come. Flowers came that morning with a card saying "At times like this, think of us first," signed Charlie Sirois, "Thinking of you at While A While Real Estate in Bosky Dells, A Good Little Town To Stay In!" The women of the village came to call, or sent their kids over holding hot casseroles between oven mitts or pies in Tupperware with messages from their mothers. "Mom said to tell you she's . . . , " etc. The police came, questioned her, left, returned, questioned her some more. Brought the silver purse, laid the moldy contents on the clean kitchen table. She fingered through them, read each card, looked at the ticket, held the lipstick, identified the emerald ring, nodded, wept a little, blew her nose. "She's taking it real well, real well," everyone said, including the police who had lunch at the lunch counter. "A real lady," the police said. "Not many left like her. Take it from me. She's taking it real well."

The envelope taped to the cash register filled up a little, not much. Glinda, who had always thought of herself as a "legend," would be miffed to see how few people remembered her, at least with a cash contribution. Too many folks had just moved to town and didn't know her at all; the old-timers who knew her back then were dead themselves or else, like Buzz and Harold, unable to contribute much. The store clerk who emptied the envelope every night and put the proceeds into another envelope marked "True" in the safe, would count the day's take and estimate two undecorated wreaths, at most; too bad.

Good as his word, tireless Snooky—with Father Kildare's lengthy, detailed, and reiterated advice—managed everything. The walker thumped nonstop these days, but Snooky kept running into the parlor, grateful for guidance. No church service possible, they decided. Father Kildare did not think he would be welcome doing any kind of service at the Baptist Church. There was no funeral parlor in town. The Masonic Hall was centrally located, and its meeting room big enough, but Glinda had been a Catholic (or so she used to say) so that was out, of course. The Catholic Church which might welcome—or at least tolerate—Father Kildare doing the service, was a summer chapel only (brown, shingled, cottage style), but no one in town knew who had the key, so that was useless. A tasteful graveside service, concluded Father Kildare. A tasteful graveside service. Perfectly acceptable, this day and age. We'll use the real Prayer Book, too, he added. "From dust to dust," he thought, was particularly appropriate under the sad circumstances; but he wondered, given the sad circumstances, whether any mention of "ashes" would be tasteful at all. Snooky wasn't sure.

Meanwhile, taking care of the rest of it, Snooky called the State Liquor Store and asked them to save him six bottles of decent sherry. ("Right," they said, "we'll make a note of it.") He'd get Gerald to pick them up for him. He dusted and cleaned the house, used the vacuum in the front hall. He brushed his gray suit, sniffed for any trace of mothballs, found a navy polka-dot bow tie, but, worried that it was too loud, kept searching for his black one. He located a large-print 1928 Book of Common Prayer on the parlor shelves and propped it open to "The Order for the Burial of the Dead" on Father's lunch tray and said, "Get to work."

He made many phone calls. He tried to stay calm so he could be useful. He tried to think of his own well-being, a little. For several days, he and the Padre lived on frozen gourmet dinners which Snooky heated and scooped out into real dishes. Pussums wouldn't touch the leftovers, seemed to be in a funk, and hardly left his basket. But for once, Snooky didn't have time for an argument with Pussums. Potted shrimp? Crab? Egg salad? Too soggy? Cucumber and dill weed and a spoon of sour cream? Too summery? A cold roast, sliced thin. Crackers. A pound cake? Nothing too colorful for after a funeral, he decided. Just plain, and preferably white. Or gray. Some of that slivered turkey breast? Determined not to resort to paper, he spent a morning searching every closet and finally did locate the shoe box with twenty-four ironed damask napkins, cocktail sized, a little yellowed, but who had time to wash and starch and iron them now? Would there be more than twenty-four people?

To everything the townsfolk did, said, cooked, offered, and to all of Snooky's plans (which he updated in a phone call every few minutes), Adele simply nodded and looked grateful. Stunned, but grateful.

To everything the police explained to her, Adele nodded. At first they wanted a delay, no funeral yet. She nodded. The Rescue Squad explained what they knew to the police, and the police told her, and Rescue came over and told her what they'd told the police, and she nodded. Buzz was questioned by everyone, and he came to tell Adele what he had told them, and how bad he felt about it.

The police wrote everything down and used words like "forensic" and "coroner" and "reports" and "delays" and she nodded.

Rescue explained to everyone what they'd heard and seen, being first on the spot. Of course there was much speculation, in town, about who could've done it. But someone always corrected, "who could've done what?" Was this, in other words, a murder? No marks on the body. Then again, no body. "Earth Angel," said Gerald, "had prolly been a mistake on account've it was dark." And what about clues? How could a backhoe find clues, for God's sake? This murmur got back to the police who began (in the privacy of the heated cruiser) to wonder if they'd done the right thing giving Buzz permission to use heavy equipment. The police consoled each other with the reality that the dump would have been chockablock with clues: metal, blood, fur, hammer handles, scraps of insinuating letters, empty pesticide bottles, weedkillers, spent bullets from shooting rats, rusty blades, bones, footprints, tire tracks, tires.

It was positively hopeless, they consoled each other. The dump, you could say, was composed of nothing *but* clues. They couldn't even prove "foul play," they told Adele. She nodded. The skeleton, they went on, had no marks at all, that is, of ax wounds or suspicious rust or bullet holes and all. It was "marked" (they didn't tell her this), but from having spent twenty-five or -six years resting on a rusted white-gas can and next to a set of twin bedsprings. A toe was missing. Toe bones. Third toe, right foot. Someone at the Store said "those goddamn rats" out loud, but got a dirty look. Perhaps (one officer speculated to the other) the victim had overindulged, at the dump, passed out, been accidentally covered up by a load next morning. "Makes sense," said the other officer. "Sure, truck would've backed in, couldn't of seen anything lying there, just dumped his load and left."

"Yes, she'd left," nodded Adele. "We'd never been what you might call close. When she left she said I'd see her when I saw her, I believe is what she said. 'You'll see me when you see me, Adele,' she said. And no, I've never heard from her again, but she never was much for writing, and as I say, we weren't what you'd call close. She wasn't much for family, you know. Well, no, you wouldn't know. But, she wasn't. No, I wasn't surprised. Good riddance to bad . . . well, good riddance, I have always thought. Until now, naturally. I don't mind telling you that we never really did get along that well. But, not even a Christmas card once in a while? You'd think a card at Christmas, wouldn't you!"

This time, the officers nodded. After several more days of delays, experts, and consultation, writing in their notebooks, asking the same questions of the same people, talking on the cruiser phone, and interviewing Gerald and the rest of Rescue for the umpteenth time, the police declared Glinda True's death "accidental," and released the bones for reburial. Adele nodded, and felt some amount of relief.

Because of the official delay, Snooky's supply of funeral sherry had dwindled to five bottles, but he thought that would be enough. He fed the first loaves of sandwich bread to the birds and cut the crusts off new loaves and stacked those slices under damp towels in the refrigerator, but anything for Adele, he told everyone else on the phone, anything to save poor Adele from having to think.

At the end of five days, the Store had done a land-office business, though they thought they'd probably lost money on coffee refills. The town scarcely had time to consider things for itself because it stayed so busy passing along every updated scrap over the scanner, by phone, or in cars parked side by side. Snooky could hardly stay on his feet, but did. The Ladies Auxiliary decided to "see how things go, for awhile," so there were no plans for a benefit supper.

The out-of-town hearse had collected the bones from the police basement and taken them to the out-of-town funeral parlor. Gerald was being awfully good about everything, picking up the sherry, going to the supermarket, answering questions, driving Snooky and Adele to the funeral parlor to choose the casket, smoking in the car while they went inside—not feeling himself properly next of kin. Snooky and Adele consulted a long time with the director of the funeral parlor—parlor or home—odd words for it, Gerald thought, practicing smoke rings against the windshield. "Something nice," was all Adele could say, so the details were left to Snooky.

Maple. Interior? The director showed them a color chart of velvet swatches, and slowly, sadly, dirgelike, read off the colors as he carefully turned the pages: Sandstone. Beige. Eggshell. Light Pink. Rose Beige. Bone. Moonstone. "Any plain white?" asked Snooky. "Oh no, we never use dead white," said the director. "It's just too hard to work with, you know what I mean? You take stark white, as far as putting somebody against that, it just bleaches everything right out. So, we stick to these neutrals, we call them. Unless, of course, the loved ones want a special interior, in which case there'd be a delay." Snooky picked Rose Beige; Adele nodded. They left, Snooky holding Adele's elbow.

The funeral director and his employees puzzled over what to do, the right thing to do, and had ended up laying the undressed bones very gently into the soft pink-velvet interior and closing the lid. No visiting hours; certainly no viewing. "Takes all kinds," the director kept saying, "takes all kinds." But he wasn't sure if he was referring to Adele, or to Snooky, or to the corpse.

Meantime, deer season had opened, so though the police felt kind of uncomfortable about the whole bones business, they certainly had enough new stuff to worry about, starting off opening day with the accidental killing of a rich, old, unmarried guy from New Jersey who'd gone out with two nephews, unemployed, local, both of whom swore they hadn't fired a shot.

The sun rose later and set a few minutes earlier, but it suddenly seemed much darker than it should be, much earlier. Because the Store was also the "official weighing station," and the scales were outside, blood replaced smashed pumpkins in the street. A tally for bucks, for does, was taped next to the envelope in memory of Glinda. To whatever somebody said to her, Adele nodded. The town began, a little, to lose interest, and "got your deer yet?" replaced talk of the murder at the dump. By the day of the graveside service, Adele was dead tired. Getting dressed these past mornings, answering the phone, answering the back door, accepting the

Tupperware containers of potato salad and jello, nodding to police, trying to keep the story straight, and listening to Snooky change plans, had been about as much as she could handle.

Meanwhile, no living Glinda, no real Glinda showed up. Adele just wanted to get this over with. She was sick to death, almost, of having to act sad, of having to pretend to be strong, of pink-lined caskets, of Glinda, and yes, as much as she wouldn't admit it, even a little sick of Snooky. Not that she didn't appreciate all he had done, and especially for the nice sandwiches, and the ironed napkins, and the four bottles of sherry, and all the rest of it, but she honestly didn't know how much longer she could keep all this up, all this mourning. So many strange things going on. Like the cleaning lady. Snooky had arranged for, of all things, a cleaning lady to come to her house yesterday.

For years he had been saying to her, "You really must get some help, Darling. It's just too much for you with the shop and all." But of course she never had. It just wasn't in her to let someone into her house—to wash things, to dust, to poke in her drawers and closets. Until yesterday morning when Snooky had called almost at dawn and said sweetly in his "I don't know if you're going to be mad at me" voice, "I've hired a house person coming at eight. Now don't argue. It's my treat, Dear Heart, and you certainly don't need to worry about a clean house At A Time Like This. And you don't have to thank me because friends never have to thank friends for caring, do they?"

So, an unwelcome Mrs. Mott had arrived, luckily from some other town, and not exactly at 8:00, more like 8:45, and had proceeded to disrupt and disarrange the whole house while Adele sat in the living room and watched soap operas she'd never seen before. Mrs. Mott talked to herself, scrubbed surfaces with Murphy's Oil Soap, scolded Fido, and used strong disinfectant in the tub. Then she packed her duffel bag and left without a word to Adele the whole time. After she had gone, Adele opened the doors and wandered around the house rearranging the cups on the sideboard and straightening the candlesticks and all the photographs on the walls. What she really wanted to do was go across the street and open up the shop, but she knew that wouldn't look right. About one o'clock, a huge bunch of gladiolas arrived in a florist's van, and then Snooky called again, just as she was lying down for a nap.

"I saw the delivery truck and I can see the glads on the table from the window. I just wanted to know you were enjoying them, and then I want you to take a wee nap, just for me, will you?"

Adele agreed, thanked him, left the phone off the hook and curled up on the guest-room bed with Fido, where both slept until it was dark.

Now, the afternoon of the graveside service, she was searching in her small closet for something to wear. For appearance sake, it had to be dark, and certainly not flashy or gay. The gray suit, perhaps? Well, a little snug. Shrunk at the cleaners, darn that cleaners. Black dress? No, she could not be that hypocritical, not even for Snooky. She finally decided on the medium brown skirt and matching jacket. Nice and fallish. With a tan blouse. Though she would have preferred her red blouse, which said a lot about mourning Glinda if, in fact, this charade even was. Adele laid the clothes on her bed and went to take a bath.

The graveside service was set for 3:30. A light rain fell, almost a mist, almost a fog. A little after three o'clock, Gerald pulled up in front of the Rectory and helped Snooky load Father Kildare into the front of the cruiser.

"Just ease on in there, Reverend. I'll put the walker in back, no prob." Snooky fussed, arranged a wool shawl over Father Kildare's thin legs.

"We don't have to potty first, do we?" he asked. "There's no place at the cemetery, you know."

Father Kildare grunted and stared ahead, clutching the heavy prayer book. "Ready?" said Gerald.

Snooky nodded, got in the back seat, and they set off to drive a few yards to Adele's back door.

When she heard the car outside, Adele sighed with relief. This is almost over. Just a few more hours. Then I can go over to the shop again. I can feel that it's not sinful to get hungry at least once a day. I can get back to normal. She didn't even give Gerald time to come to the door before she was halfway down the walk headed for the car.

"Climb in, dear," Snooky said. "The whole back seat for us," and he patted the vinyl upholstery of the cruiser. She got in and Gerald shut the door.

"Oh, your brown suit," Snooky said. "A very good choice. More modern. I was hoping you wouldn't wear the black dress. Black makes you look so drawn and all eyes will be on you today, you know, Old Thing." He tugged on the coat of his gray jacket and smoothed a wrinkle in his pants.

"You look very nice, too," Adele said.

The road to the cemetery was lined with cars, but of course Gerald could drive right through, the blinker on his car flashing cheerfully. He parked beside the hearse, and after helping Adele out first, and then helping Snooky unpack Father Kildare and the walker, he went to stand next to the funeral director in the background.

Adele glanced at the shiny casket, dotted with raindrops, sitting alongside the open grave. She tried not to think of what lay inside. She saw Buzz standing off to one side under a dripping tree, and held out her hand to him. He came forward and took it. She held out her other hand to Snooky, but he shook his head and leaned forward and whispered, "Be strong, love. He needs you, and of course you know you've *got* me."

Buzz's thin face was gray and there was a dab of dried blood on his chin. His suit, though a little short, was clean, pressed. His eyes were red-rimmed, and his shoulders drooped.

It seemed like the whole town was there. Puck stood next to Wilma Look, under an umbrella. He was wearing a green suit, a kind of mixture of lime and moss. "They can all wear black if they want to," he had told anybody who'd listen, "but I'm sure as hell not going to. Glinda wasn't a black kind of gal, let me tell you, and

I can assure you I knew her real well, real well." Every time he said this, Wilma sniffed and looked away. Harold stood on the edges of the crowd, under a big pine tree, his hands jammed in the pockets of his old brown pants. He kept glancing towards the woods as if assuring himself that an avenue of escape was open. This was Harold's third funeral. He had gone to his mother's, and then to Gunther Kringle's, but this one seemed more important than either of those because so many people were here.

Father Kildare coughed into his hand and the crowd fell silent. He paused, took a breath. Snooky watched him anxiously, afraid that the old man might topple over; but then, in a burst of love, Snooky could see him rally. This was not the feeble old Padre who clomped for his supper and clomped for his paper and clomped for his Ovaltine. This was the beautiful priest Snooky had first seen, so many years ago, intoning vespers in the school chapel. "He is magnificent," Snooky thought with pride hurting his heart. He felt his eyes smarting. "The old devil," he thought.

Adele and Buzz held hands, and the rain misted down, and overhead a crow cawed sharply in the drizzly light. Father Kildare opened the big book of large print and began to read:

> I am the resurrection and the life, saith the Lord: he that believeth in me, though he were dead, yet shall he live: and whosoever liveth and believeth in me, shall never die.
>
> I know that my redeemer liveth, and that he shall stand at the latter day upon the earth: and though this body be destroyed, yet shall I see God: whom I shall see for myself, and mine eyes shall behold, and not as a stranger.

❋ ❋ ❋ ❋

Glinda True glanced at the speedometer of her new (new to her) red Mercury Capri convertible: 75 mph, and smooth as silk. November be damned, she had the top down, the wind in her hair, and Lyle Lovett crooning to her from the car's CD. Glinda tried to envision Lyle sitting beside her right now, his wild crop of hair blowing in the country wind. "Country Wind," what a great name for a song that would be, she thought.

"You love the boy with the pretty green eyes," Lyle sang; green eyes, blue eyes, what does it matter? She'd spend a week in Hell for one hour with ole Lyle. "She wasn't good, but she had good intentions," he purred. Well, her intentions might not be the best, but she was good. Glinda laughed. An hour with Lyle would be worth two weeks in Hell.

But even a whole night with Lyle wouldn't be enough to entice her to spend one minute longer than she had to in Bosky Dells. Fifteen more miles. Thank God the rain had stopped, at least. What a Godforsaken hick town. Nobody in Bosky Dells ever got out, at least not alive. Not Adele, not Puck, not Buzz, probably. Sure, they'd dreamed about getting out. Back in high school, Buzz used to say that someday he'd buy a silver Corvette and drive to California, to Oregon. Buzz. The Dump Man of the Sticks. And Adele. Good old Adele. What a raging fake. Then there was Puck. Of course, maybe Puck had escaped. Puck was no fool. He liked being a goose in a duck pond, Glinda thought. Actually, of everyone in town she could remember, she probably liked Puck best. Maybe he was still there. Still unmarried? Maybe she'd give him a call tonight. A week was a long, long time in a haystack like this one, and a week was the amount of time she planned to be there, not one second more.

She had planned to get this over with about five days ago. But these damned car dealers. "Not refreshed in time," they told her, "just another coupla days, sorry about this." Glinda hated to be late, hated to have this stupid trip hung up. Well, at least this would give the simple folks of the sticks something to think about. The day Glinda True was late.

She pushed on the accelerator. Boy, this little kitten could purr. Almost there. She nearly didn't see the man standing beside the road, waving with both hands. A dark small car was pulled off on the shoulder. Damn. Well, she ought to stop. She had no fear of picking up a stranger, but, she'd be obligated to give him a ride. What a pain. Glinda screeched to a halt, slammed the Capri into reverse, and backed up in a cloud of exhaust.

Oh, hell. She couldn't believe it. He had "cop" written all over him. He peered in her window through his wire-rimmed glasses.

She rolled it down, began to get her story ready. "Lucky for you," he said, "I'm off duty."

"I'm always lucky," Glinda said. "What's wrong with your car?"

The man frowned. "It's gone. Dead. Kaput. And I don't know what's wrong."

"Well, hop in. I'll give you a ride to town, drop you at the garage. Where you headed?"

"Little place not far called Bosky Dells. Partridge hunting. If you can hang on a minute, I'll get my stuff from the car. I sure appreciate this. I'm booked at the Night Roost Bed & Breakfast. Ever hear of it?"

"I've heard of it. Come on. Going to Bosky Bozo myself, visiting a cousin."

"Thanks," he said, opened the back door and stowed his bag, then got into the front, propping the gun at his side. A double, side-by-side Purdy 16-gauge. To Glinda, it was just a real nice looking gun. She openly checked out its owner. Tall, reddish brown hair. The wire-rimmed glasses. A wool jacket. Kind of lanky, but not badly built.

"Nice gun," she said.

"Real nice," he said. "The name's Celted, Liam Celted, hard 'c'. Detective with Boston PD. Like I said, you're lucky I'm off duty."

Glinda laughed. A real empty threat. This drip wasn't even from the state. Well, she'd play along.

"New car," she said, "you know how it is. Sorry, though."

"Actually, traffic tickets aren't what you'd call my specialty. Taking a few days off. One of the fellows on the desk told me about this place, Bosky Dells, he's got an aunt there. Said the hunting was really fine. By the way, don't you think it's a little late in the season to have the top down?"

"I live dangerously." Glinda gradually pushed harder on the gas.

"So, what's your business in Bosky Dells?"

"I used to live here. Like I said, I'm visiting my cousin. Just for a few days. How long you planning to be here?" (Shit. A sharp cop could screw up her plans.)

"A week, that's all."

Glinda scowled. As if the local boys in blue weren't bad enough.

The Mercury had a mind of its own. Seventy, and the cop wasn't noticing. Seventy-five, and he didn't blink. Eighty, and on a curve the gun fell against his leg. "Take it easy, little lady," Celted said. She dropped back to seventy, and they rode in silence.

Around a turn, the dark woods on one side of the narrow road, a gray lake on the other, Glinda suddenly braked in front of a huge white house with a twenty-foot rooster on the front lawn.

"Your destination," she said. "'The World Famous Night Roost.' Good luck."

Celted squinted at the house, at the rooster, at the house. "Doesn't look like there's anyone at home," he said. Glinda had to agree. The yard was empty of cars; the windows were without lights.

"Let's go see," she said. "I used to know these people anyhow; could say hello as long as I'm in town." She got out of the car.

They went up the cement walk, lined with blackened geraniums. Glinda opened the oak door and stuck her head in.

"Hello?" she yelled. "Gladys? Bert? you here?" But the inn could have changed hands in the years she had been gone. Maybe she was calling the wrong names. Oh, not likely. There was no answer, though, no sign of any life.

"Look," Celted said, pointing to a sign hanging off the nose of the moose head mounted over the fireplace. "Gone to the funeral," it read, "back at 5. Pls. make yourself to home." A funeral. Who could have died? Jeez, just about anybody or nobody. Maybe Buzz, or Puck. Christ, maybe Adele. What a godsend that would be. It would be too much.

"Let's go," she said. "I'll drop you at the garage."

In town it was obvious to her, though maybe not to Celted, that everything was shut down, deserted. Like a ghost town. The Store was closed with the same sign: Gone to a Funeral. Re-open

4:30. She saw a sign on a tacky little gift shop—About Thyme—God, could anybody be so corny? "Closed Due To Death In Imm. Family," it read. The garage was closed, another sign.

"Well, hell's bells," she said, "we could try the cemetery, I guess. This oughta be interesting."

How far was the cemetery, anyhow? Was this even the right road? Yep, right road. Past the dump on the left, cemetery next lane to the right. Raining again. She pulled over, pushed a button, the top slid into place. Hard to see. The rain, the grayness.

The long line of parked cars and trucks slowed Glinda down a bit. Whoever had died sure had a following. Nothing to do but sit in the car and wait, or else park and walk in the rain. She pulled in behind the last car. For a few minutes they sat there, listening to the steady patter.

"No point in sitting here alone," she said to Celted. "Let's go see who died."

Together, slanted into the rain, they began the walk down the cemetery road. Up ahead, Glinda could see a crowd of people huddled in a circle. Looked like everybody in town. Finally she could make out Adele, she thought. Though wow, Adele looked old. And was that Buzz alongside her, half bald? Looked like it. She and Celted drew closer.

Dog was under a juniper bush, trying to stay dry, when he spotted the two strangers approaching. Buzz had told him, "All right, if you want to go you can go, but you gotta stay out of the way and you gotta be quiet." "Be quiet," stayed in Dog's mind. But he didn't know these people walking towards him. And they were rapidly coming up on the people he did know. He began to bark a warning. Buzz turned to shush him, stared at the people, sucked in his breath, and dropped Adele's hand. Father Kildare was reading "in sure and certain hope of the Resurrection unto eternal life," and Adele turned to see why Buzz had dropped her hand. She stared, and then screamed. Or howled. Very unlike her, thought Snooky, who also turned, as did everyone else. Father Kildare went on to the end, oblivious. Harold was the only one listening. The crow called overhead; Dog barked louder. Harold turned, saw the blond woman and the strange man, and, in absolute terror of he knew not what, fled into the darkening woods.

END OF PART I

PART II
Chapter V

Adele

The house, except for various ticks and creaks, is totally quiet. It is ten o'clock in the morning, four days after "the funeral." Adele sits in her plaid bathrobe and fuzzy slippers at her kitchen table, drinking her fourth cup of tea. She has not raised the shades, or fed the stove, and it is cold in the house. Though the phone has rung twice, she has not answered it. Fido is nowhere to be seen or heard.

Glinda is still asleep in the back bedroom. Her faint ragged snores can be heard, now and then, from where Adele is sitting in the kitchen. Even without raising the shade, Adele knows it is another gray, drizzly day.

The coffee crowd at the Store has gathered, and early-morning hunters are coming in with their kill. The weighing scale is hooked up outside, a few feet away from the Store's front door, and four days of rainy mist has washed the deer blood everywhere. The smell of fur, blood, rain, and engines running, has by now replaced the smell of burning tires, smashed pumpkins, and kerosene.

The sign Snooky made, "Closed Due To Death In Imm. Family" still hangs from the doorknob of About Thyme, but now it is washed out and faded and looks as though it's been hanging there for months, not days. Adele knows there will be no more tourists wanting souvenirs for many months now, but still, she ought to be unpacking the Christmas stock and opening the shop for winter hours. She knows this, but sits there at the table. The thought of the cold shop, smelling of dust and mice and dry rot and blueberry soap, somehow sickens her.

Many years ago, the "body" was buried. Now, many years later, it is "dug up." Then a new hole is dug for it, in a proper place. The "body" is placed in a "casket" and is minutes from going back into the ground. Sanctified this time, not dumped or hidden. The re-burial will be slow at first (the long sentences of the service, hand-fuls of ceremonial sod and a few blossoms), and then, when every-one has gone back down the hill in the dark afternoon, some to Snooky's house for sandwiches and sherry and cake and coffee, "it" will be covered up quickly and efficiently by the assistants of the funeral-home director. When they are finished, they will place the undecorated wreaths, bought with the money left "in memory" at the Store, on the mud of the fresh grave. The wreaths will make an odd Christmasy touch. And, in fact, because they will stay green, they won't need to be replaced at Christmas. Which would save Adele a trip to the cemetery in a few weeks. Adele had thought about all this; that is, before the funeral was so unfortunately brought to a dead halt.

Glinda was certainly alive and she was certainly here. Her red car sat in the driveway Her cosmetics were all over the bathroom. Her high-heeled boots with zippers were still where she'd flung them down last night. Absurd shoes, with winter coming. But Glinda never had much sense. This was certainly her, though.

The funeral director knew the "body" was certainly not Glinda True. Everyone could see that for themselves. The "body," whoever it was, was back in the police morgue. The pink-lined casket, empty, closed, was also in the police station, off to one side in a basement hallway. This was a difficulty. In a sense, it was a "used" casket, even though, of course, it had not been used for long. Adele had paid for it, paid in cash, paid in full. So the funeral director was not worried about that part of it. He didn't know what they'd now do with the remains, again, but whatever it was, he just prayed he wouldn't be involved. Nor did he (nor anyone else) know exactly who "they" might be. Until it was known who "it" was, "they" was also up for grabs. Unless by "they" you meant the police, not relatives or somebody.

Meanwhile, no one else had died, so the director had time to think. Somehow, he thought he felt offended by all this, but couldn't put his finger on quite why. Something about the normal order of things, he thought. Think of all the things that had been skipped. Well, naturally, they hadn't been necessary. Embalming, for one. A nice outfit, for another. Make-up. The guest book. Miss True hadn't even wanted the guest book at the after-funeral lunch; said she knew everyone who was there. What kind of thinking was that? The tape of organ playing hadn't been needed, or the new yellow-shaded lights. His boys had done a fine job, though; a credit to the firm.

Nice boys, the boys who worked at the funeral home. Always looked nice, too, in their dark year-round suits. Not many women went into this business, he thought. Wonder why? God knows women can do anything they want, these days. But it just wouldn't look right—a woman in a dark year-round suit, standing by the entrance, pressing hands and taking elbows. Odd what you think of sometimes. Although he knew that what he buried, in proper order, eventually, somewhere down the line, became bones, he'd never been in charge of burying the end product before this. It involved a lot more headaches than somebody might think.

And then that God-awful scene at the cemetery. People screaming, fainting, laughing, running into the woods, cops, more cops, a traffic jam, horns honking, some ancient Catholic minister reading out of some ancient book, half-wits, dogs, confusion, rain, mud, he'd never seen anything like it, not in his entire career. Of course Bosky Dells had always been a Godforsaken weirdo place, and he was glad he didn't live there, didn't have to do much business there. He was glad to close his office for lunch and walk down to a decent restaurant. Nice to live in a real honest-to-God town, he thought. But, what was he worried about?

He worried, and felt lousy about it, that Adele True might now try to get him to take back the casket, and ask for a refund. He felt bad because that morning he'd had to make out the bill for the "funeral," or whatever the hell you wanted to call it, and send it to her. He had tried to figure out if the cousin who was supposed to be getting buried but then showed up ought to get the bill, but then the whole thing wasn't her fault, was it?

But then, really, it wasn't anybody's fault, but he had to make a living, didn't he? The other Miss True, the one who was alive, well, no, that wasn't right. Miss Adele—the one who had ordered the casket—she seemed so nice and all, he hated to do this. After all, she had made an honest mistake, he supposed. He could take the coffin back again, and—perhaps with a small discount—give Miss Adele back her money. Of course he couldn't resell it, but he might be able to use it for display. Against the law to sell a used casket; he knew that, but until now, had never thought about why. He didn't know. Shit, what a mess. He could "clean" the coffin and give it away to some needy person, maybe. Maple, too. Not the priciest, but up there. But who, in the future, would want a somewhat used coffin, casket (he always corrected himself), for a departed beloved? Either way, any way, he stood to lose. If Miss Adele kept the coffin, he'd feel a little cheap. Not that he could help what the law said. But if they—Miss Adele—returned the casket, he was bound to lose money. But (he consoled himself) losing was the very nature of this business. He locked his office door and went out for lunch.

Still hunched at her table over toast scraps and cold tea bags, Adele also thought about the expensive casket and wondered— since the whole thing was, in a big way, her fault—if she could have the nerve to ask the funeral home to take it back. Gerald would probably do it for her, so that was no problem. Or, maybe the funeral home would just bring the hearse out again and collect it themselves. Well, for that matter, where exactly was it? A tidy sum, she kept thinking, a tidy sum, and certainly a waste if it doesn't get used. Do police keep unsolved murder victims forever? That is, until the case is solved? In which case, would the police get tired of tripping over the pink-lined coffin and just take it to the dump? What a waste.

Adele thought of herself as normally thrifty, not tight, and God knows, not stingy. I'm careful, that's all, she thought. I'm careful, and I was raised to be careful, and that's the way it is. I reuse tea bags. I save leftovers. I don't throw good money after bad. I don't keep this house blazing hot every minute. I mend my clothes. I buy cat food on sale. I save on the electric by turning out the lights when I leave the room. And, I . . . don't feel like letting a perfectly good coffin go to waste. (Though I know someone I'd be willing to use it for, she thought. Then stifled the thought.)

Adele is fifty-odd years old (she never has occasion to say exactly), and she has lived in this house just about her whole life. She has always looked fifty-odd, even as a child. Even at fourteen or fifteen, she had no bosom, and what she had rode low. Her hair was mouse-colored and she had no waist and it was already clear that she'd have a big bum and skinny stemmy legs. In fact, from a pew or two behind, she and her grandmother, standing together to share a hymnal, looked just alike except for the color of hair and, sometimes, color of coat.

Her parents were dead. She had no memory of them, only remembered living with Gram and Gramps in this house, with this clock, this table, these green pull shades, with the smell of woodsmoke, tea bags, mothballs, and wet wintry things, like felt liners from boots.

The three of them ate the food she eats now—toast, beans, sardines, canned corn chowder, and, sometimes, gray furry roast beef. Fiddleheads in spring, with mayonnaise; stewed tomatoes; boiled dinners year-round; hash. A gift company sent a tea sampler to her shop, and Adele tried the Lapsang Souchong and liked it, so she has added that to the menu, but still keeps Red Rose on hand. And, she has added two or three bottles of rum a year, no more. Sometimes, on cold afternoons, she and Snooky add a spoonful to their tea.

The bathroom towels and mats are still good, and so are the sheets and covers. The furniture, protected from the sun by the green shades, and covered by various shawls, throws, afghans, slipcovers, and doilies, is still good. Certainly good enough for many more years, so are the throw rugs.

She still wears her grandmother's nightgowns. To bring in the wood, she wears an old jacket of her grandfather's. Her grandmother had liked nice things, and kept them, unused, in her bureau. Thus Adele often thought that her grandmother would have liked the various items for sale in About Thyme, and would have made a bar of cranberry soap last for years by never unwrapping it and tucking it under the slips, nightgowns, and bed jackets she was saving. What was she saving them for?

Adele went to the grade school, to church, and on holidays to the cemetery with her grandparents. They went to the cemetery on the Saturday before Easter, on the Sunday before Memorial Day, and once again the week before Christmas. All the family, on both sides, was buried there. Later, Adele went to the district high school, and though she was not popular, she made good grades, good enough, and graduated eighth in her class. Under her photo in the yearbook it said—"Works hard! Loyal friend! Good business student. Bound to succeed!" She had thought so, too.

So, with prompting and encouragement from her typing teacher, she entered business school the following fall. It was only half an hour from home, so she could learn bookkeeping and improve her shorthand, but still be at home every night to help with supper and chores. Plus it was only a two-year program, so Gram wouldn't have to do everything around the house without Adele's help for very long. She caught a ride every day with a carpool and chipped in for gas. She herself never learned to drive.

During her second year at school, when she was taking Office Management and Advanced Accounting, three things happened. These things changed the course of her life and, now that she looks back on it, ruined her chances for broader horizons. The first was that one day bringing in an armload of wood, Gramps fell over dead, right at the backdoor. The second was that Gram never really recovered, but became sick and stayed sick for years. The third was that the care of Gram—and Glinda—fell to Adele. Because of all this responsibility, Adele quit business school with only a few months left before her degree.

Gram and Gramps had raised two sons. Adele's father (and her mother) died of flu, and that's when Adele, just a tot, came to stay.

Glinda's father (and her mother) died in a car wreck when Glinda was fourteen (and Adele seventeen), and so Glinda, having no other relatives who could take her, came to live with Gram and Gramps, too.

If you could turn Adele upside down and rearrange her various parts, you'd get Glinda. Glinda was just right. Instead of big hips and tiny breasts, she had small hips and big breasts, even at fourteen She was blond, and she had a waistline. She was wild. She was new in town. She laughed a lot. She wore short flippy skirts, tight sweaters, and lipstick which she applied while on the school bus because Gram wouldn't let her leave the house with it on. Unlike Adele's clothes, which were tan, navy, brown, and too big, Glinda's clothes were red, pink, turquoise, yellow, and too small. She had angora sweater sets and penny loafers, a winter coat with a hood, a see-through umbrella with kittens on it, a charm bracelet, a little hard suitcase of make-up, magazines, and white cotton bras that she washed and starched herself. She became a cheerleader. She plucked her eyebrows. She washed her hair in Halo, and, while it was in curlers, she read her movie magazines.

Though Adele was three years older, Glinda treated Adele from the beginning as though Adele were a lot younger, slightly retarded, and a drip. She gave Adele fashion "hints" (or read them aloud to her), and said things like: "you need to get out more! Lose some of that weight! Boys would like you if you learned to use make-up, you know. Get a perm, for pity's sake! Look, lick your lips, then rub this on with your finger. Can't you hitch up those straps? Adele, if you just fixed yourself up, you wouldn't be half bad. Hey, wanna hear what I found out last night? Sit down here on the bed and let me tell you what happened to Buzz in the car; God, you wouldn't believe! Did you know that kind of thing happened? I mean, I didn't let him go all the way, Adele, don't be fruity. I only let him touch my bra, promise, but then. . . ."

And then Gram would call from her bedroom down the hall, and though Adele wanted to know—a little—what happened when Buzz mauled Glinda's bra, she also thought it was pretty disgusting, and so was glad to have to leave the room and take care of

Gram. "Save me," she sometimes prayed at night. But she wasn't sure from what, exactly.

Then Adele fell in love. Not with Buzz or Puck or any of the other gawky boys at the high school, but with an older man, a foreign man, a beautiful man with a beautiful voice and lovely eyes and hands—Mr. Kringle, Gunther—who bought the house next door and moved to town. Her love for him began as curiosity (having never met a foreign person before), turned to a kind of motherly pity (he lived all alone, no wife or children), then to a crush (and dreams), and then to love. Then the love became quite fierce and stayed that way for many years, all the way up to the time of his death and beyond. Even now, years later, he is her "love" in a way no one else has ever been, in a way Snooky could never be, close as they are, and is her "love" in the sense that she has never felt those particular feelings again, at all.

To Gunther Kringle, she was the little girl next door he sometimes patted on the hair, always spoke to if he saw her in the yard, and to whom he occasionally lent a book or for whom he occasionally played an album of opera. Rather, he would hand her the album of *Cosi Fan Tutte* or *Tristan und Isolde* and show her how to work the turntable. He would go about his business, and Adele, the passionate high-school senior, would sit in what is now Snooky's front parlor, pressing the album cover to her chest, staring through the vine that covered the bay window, and listen to the arias. At Christmas, or if he heard it was her birthday, he gave her small, inexpensive pieces of jewelry in white boxes. Once, a silver heart on a too-short chain; once, a bracelet with three seed pearls on a bangle. She still had the jewelry; she still had the boxes. Only just before he died did he chance to notice the deep nature of her attentions and the doglike look in her pretty eyes. By then, however, so much else had happened, it was too late to undo her crush. And then he died so unexpectedly.

Naturally, Glinda caught on to Adele's crush at once, and told her it was "truly disgusting" and that the books were "weird" and the music "weirder." Gram just thought it was "nice" for Mr. Kringle to take an interest, and Gramps didn't notice anything at all to do with the two girls or with "that feller" next door. Thus, unwittingly, Glinda and the grandparents provided exactly the climate in which a passionate love is safe: taunts, misunderstanding, and obliviousness.

So Adele didn't mind too much when she had to quit business school, even though her daily life then became bedpans, washing, ironing, sweeping, bringing in wood, mashing things for Gram to eat, changing sheets, getting to church, paying the bills, reading a little at night—in bed—mystery stories, Gunther's art books, *Jane Eyre* from the Library, which she checked out again and again. Glinda did not help with anything at all. Though Gram fretted over Glinda and made Adele keep track of her: make sure her clothes were clean, make sure she was studying, make sure she didn't stay out late.

Soon, Adele believed, she'd return to business school, take up where she'd left off, graduate, be someone's really good secretary. Someone with a business of some kind. The world was full of possibilities. She would lose some weight. She would graduate. Soon, Gunther would see she was thin and well-qualified. Meantime, despite her many chores, she still managed to see him or hear him every day, could still borrow the books and listen to his music, and—maybe best of all—watch him through his kitchen window through her kitchen window.

But, something went amiss here. At this time in her still young life, Adele seemed to stop thinking, or stop talking about herself. Or, the routine of washing, ironing, cooking, going to bed, and beginning again took over and eliminated thought and time. Or perhaps she simply got too lonely for her own good; a loneliness she didn't altogether feel because she was used to it. Circumstances conspired to leave her in too much isolation.

Thus, thought and time and self got muddled, and time began to go very quickly, even though every day was more or less exactly like the day before and the day to come. Gunther went on about his business, whatever it was, and though he was as wonderful as he had ever been, nothing got more wonderful. Gram got no better. On the other hand, she got no worse. Glinda's life—cars, boys, beer, flunked classes, summer school, boys, beer, cars, and so forth—seemed more eventful than Gram's life, or Adele's, but was actually just as unchanging and dull.

As happens more often than not, nothing happened at all. Adele's life simply stopped, though she did not know it at the time. Gram's life was going nowhere, which of course was the entire point of it. Glinda's life was always revving up but never taking off.

We say "fate," but that's rather grand and other words could be used. Life, reality, rural Maine, even romance, as at least Adele and Glinda had a romance of their lives that might be and would be and would if could. Gram's illness was her "romance." Was Adele fated to live in an odd body with mouse-colored hair and a flat chest, go to business school, have to drop out, take care of Gram, mother Glinda, fall in mad wild love with a refugee on some kind of lam who happened to own a few albums of opera and an eye for nice jewelry to give teenage girls on their birthdays? Or, is this just the arc of one life?

Like fireworks—everything gets lit, catches the spark, goes up, seems to hang in the air for a moment, all potential, and then splash, zing, explode, zow itself against the darkness. But, in the very instant of most light, they are already on their way down, and fizz, flicker, spend themselves in a speedy descent. The afterimage stays in the eye longer than it remained in the air. But some go only a little ways up, fizzle out after a pop, and disappear. Some get lit, simmer, but never go up at all. The punk was wet, or the fuse too short, or the expiration date gone by. Evidently there is one exact moment when everything is ready: punk, fuse, date, sky. Perhaps this constitutes what we call "fate."

At any rate, it's clear that Adele's life never quite took off, and today, this dreary morning, she is fifty thereabouts, is wearing a man's bathrobe, hating her cousin who is still asleep, drinking her endless cups of tarry tea, and refusing to answer the phone even though she knows perfectly well the persistent caller is Snooky, her entire lifetime's one, best, and only real true friend.

On second thought, is this merely a routine fiction? Maybe this life—Adele's somewhat typical life—*is* happening, and rather well, at that. The meaning of success can still be defined, still be questioned. Maybe mournful sexual-sociological notes and long fictional faces are bunkum. For example, how can it be called "fate" (which stands in for "tragedy") in ninety-nine cases if ninety-nine out of a hundred lives don't "go" anywhere? Where was everybody supposed to go? If everybody left, who would mind the store? And was everybody supposed to signal getting someplace by moving to another geographical spot? That is, from a small Maine village to Boston? Or, from Boston to a small Maine village?

There's another way of looking at Adele's life. She has her own house, her own business, and she is her own boss. She knows everyone in town, for whatever mixed good that is, and everyone knows her. She's still alive and very healthy and now her body suits her and her face is full of intelligence and a kind of homely grace. She has many virtues: loyalty, thrift, curiosity, good manners, a good enough business sense, and an ability to keep her own counsel when necessary. She is patriotic. She reads. She loves her cat. Her wood is under cover for winter. She is looking forward to decorating her shop for Christmas. She has a long-standing solid hatred for her cousin Glinda, which has given much satisfactory meaning to her life through the years. She lives right across the street from a general store which has just about everything you'd ever need, minus a few frills. It even has a few frills.

Though she wouldn't know the word, she has a "network"— kind Gerald, friendly Miss Look at the Library, Buzz, and so on. They leave her alone, but would be right there if any trouble arose, just as she would be for them. None of this needs to be talked about, but everyone knows it is the truth. Her days are not without pleasure of many kinds. She has enjoyed a few adventures and has had several good dreams. She can look back at a life thus far of good and faithful service. She has an old New England name. She has a best friend who lives right next door and with whom she shares nearly everything, just as he shares nearly everything with her. Both have certain privacies, which is also a pleasure. Her plaid bathrobe, though old, is warm. The cat will turn up as soon as it gets hungry. Whether or not she is able to get a refund on the unused casket, she still has money in the bank.

The next time the phone rings, she thinks she will answer it.

Chapter VI

Buzz

Buzz was headed north on I-95, going to the reservation with a full load behind. Beside him, on the cracked leather seat of the Mercedes truck, Dog snoozed, his feet and nose twitching as if in time with the radio. Buzz had it turned to the "All Country Hits" station, and the farther north he got the louder and clearer it came in. Buzz tapped his fingers, doing a little dance on the steering wheel. What a hell of a week it had been, what with the funeral and all. He was glad to be out of town.

For the trip, he was wearing his Stetson and his Jensons, something he only did when he headed north. The boots were a little too radical for town, he figured. Actually, they were a kind of secret between him and Dog. Not that Dog had actually picked out the right size and paid the bill or anything. Buzz had done that himself. But with a price tag of about $500, they had seemed extravagant to buy for himself. So he had waited until nearly his birthday, then bought them, had the clerk gift-wrap them, and do the card. Then he put the box beside his cereal bowl the night before. The little gift card (the clerk had rolled her eyes) read: "To Buzz, from Dog, Happy Birthday." Then, on the big morning, he had come down and found them there, just waiting for him.

He had been very careful to read the card, express surprise, and thank Dog, and had worn the boots on the trip so that Dog would know he really liked them. Actually, he'd worn them on the very next trip they'd made to the reservation, even though back then they still rubbed blisters on his heels. His Indian friends admired them, too, and Buzz had told Willi Rainwater that if he died,

Willi would be sure to get them. At first, after he had made this promise, Buzz was somewhat nervous, especially when Willi followed him around everywhere. But after awhile, Willi seemed to forget about it and stopped trailing him, so Buzz relaxed. These boots would last forever. So would his hat.

Buzz thought his friends were going to be mighty pleased with this current load of treasures. In the back of the truck he had the front end of a Camaro, the swing set, and the lawn mowers he loaded the day he discovered the body, as well as one wringer washer that worked perfectly (he tried it out), two banana-seat bikes—one boy, one girl—several pieces of ten-foot stockade fencing, and a brown Herculon couch with only one small rip in the arm which he figured could be covered by a doily and wouldn't even show. He had wanted to ask Adele what her plans were for the coffin, because he knew what a hit that would be with his customers, but he just didn't have the heart to do it. What did you do with a used coffin, anyhow? He knew that right now it was probably just gathering dust someplace. He hated to see good things go to waste.

West of him Buzz could see the sun setting, a smeary red in the gray November dusk. He opened a package of Twinkies he'd bought at the last truck stop. Dog, hearing the wrapper crackle, opened one eye. "Want one?" Buzz asked. Dog considered. Twinkies were not one of his favorites, and he wasn't very hungry. He closed his eye and stuck his muzzle under his hip. "Suit yourself," Buzz said, and popped the cake into his own mouth. The road stretched out before him. It could have been endless. For the first time since the "funeral," Buzz felt at peace with himself and the universe.

The funeral had really shaken him up. There he was standing alongside that muddy open grave, holding Adele's cold hand because she seemed to want him to do it, trying his best not to break down and blubber, when all of a sudden, who should come walking down the cemetery road but the dead person her very self with what turned out to be a police officer in tow. At first he wasn't sure it was her, she looked so old. But she was still blond, still had that grin, and had rushed right up to him. Then the scene got real chaotic. People screaming and talking, the service going right on, the funeral home people rushing around, and the cop. Glinda acting real pissed that no one seemed at all glad to see her, then her hearing who they all thought the body was, and then acting pissed because everyone had thought she was dead to begin with. Then more cops, and then a kind of welcome-home party at Snooky's with some really strange little sandwich things and well, just a big mess all around. Good though, that here she was back, and not dead. Well, Buzz felt glad for her, anyhow.

Ever since the funeral though, something had been nagging him. He couldn't put it into words and didn't really want to. This was something he didn't like to admit. It was that some little part of him had been relieved that Glinda was dead. Finally he'd be able to put her out of his mind forever, or at least she could become a fond memory, not a living ache. Pretty goddamn, him being the one to find her and all, but he could have gotten over that. Grisly, though. But now he felt guilty that he probably wasn't overjoyed to see her alive and walking down the road the day of her funeral. If she had been dead, then maybe he could have started his life almost over again. There were certainly things he would not change, like Dog and Earth Angel and his job in general, and his trips north and his Indian friends, and taking care of Harold, but at least he might have had a chance. A chance to do what, though, he wondered.

Buzz didn't think life had ever been easy for him. Sure, he knew that a lot of people had it a lot worse. He had his little house, his job, his friends. He doubted if anyone who mattered in town would say they didn't know and like him and respect the job he did for the town. But it didn't seem easy, and it never had.

He had been born in Bosky Dells and that gave him privileges and status. He had a running account at the Store. He could walk into the post office and ask for his mail if he'd forgotten the key to his box. He had a big family plot in the oldest section of the cemetery. He was Marshal of the Memorial Day Parade each year—him and Dog and the Mercedes—and even though he had enjoyed this honor for many years now, no one ever objected at all. He had a lot to be grateful for, and he often counted his blessings, especially when driving north at night.

He doubted that much of anybody in town even remembered his father. People who came from away, then died, and were buried somewhere else, were soon forgotten. While those who were born in town could go away forever and someone would still remember them at Christmas or in some speech or in another family member's eulogy. "Yes, she was the second cousin of Wilbur Dean, who left Bosky Dells in 1952. Wilbur was born here, if you recall."

But Buzz's father had been born in New Jersey. How he ended up in a little country town way north was something of a blur, even to Buzz, but there were fragments of a reason. The elder Noble had been a professor at a small but fancy college. He was married to a woman from another rich family. So far, so good. Then there was a little incident, very blurry—with a student on campus, was the story—and the rich wife divorced him. Professor Noble took early retirement and came north to spend the summer in the cottage of a friend. The cottage was next door on the lake to a now-gone summer hotel. The professor took his meals there. There he met Buzz's mother. Well, not his mother yet, of course. She was a waitress in the dining room. The professor had a good appetite, and something of an appetite for young things, because the girl to become Buzz's mother was just out of high school that summer. At any rate, she married the professor, or the other way around, and Buzz was born the next year, in March. "And here's our little Ides of March," his father would always say, a definitely strange thing to say, and Buzz felt a chill when his father said it. The chill eventually turned to boredom.

For whatever reason, he stayed an only child. Many people said this was a good thing because he hardly got any attention as it was, much less if there were more. However, Buzz, who would have preferred being totally ignored by his parents altogether, always hoped for a little brother or something to absorb whatever attention was coming his way. Their attention, like the "ides of March" business, was always incomprehensible to him. He was not a cold or unloving child. He lavished great affection on his animals—various puppies, cats, a hutch of rabbits, small rodents in cages—as well as on his grandmother, who genuinely seemed to care about him and who admired his homemade cages and gave him stale bread and lettuce leaves and who said things that made sense to him such as "how about some lunch?" and "isn't it about time for bed?" His father said things like "what a little maverick, must be a throwback," and his mother would say "a shoot off the old stump," and his father would reply, "you should know, my darling," and his mother would say "bastard, fucking bastard," and his father would look up from his book and say "tut-tut, now watch that silvery tongue," and his mother would storm out of the house, taking Buzz with her and leaving him at his grandmother's, who then said "how about some lunch?"

Buzz grew up a stern, quiet little boy. His mother thought his animals were smelly and she treated him as though he'd just made her acquaintance. His father spent most of his time reading or painting impressions of other paintings in a room he called his studio. When he saw Buzz, he lifted his eyebrows, pulled his glasses down to peer over them, said odd things, then laughed, and went back to his painting. He seemed to act as if Buzz would enjoy the punchline, but Buzz never understood the joke.

On rare occasions, which Buzz hated and feared, his father would feel a sort of fatherly calling and would announce that he and Buzz were taking a "men only" trip. Several of these Buzz remembered well.

Once, when he was five, they went to New Jersey to see his father's mother. Buzz remembered the long, hot, boring ride, the silence, the little jabs and ironies. Finally he must have gone to sleep in the back seat, because the next thing he recalled was being pulled from the car and told, "We're here, son of mine," and told that he'd now better "step lively for his grandmama." Buzz said, "I got to go." "Not now you don't, " his father had told him. "Go with Giles. Giles, take him. After I say hello to Mother, I'll bring her down to meet this handsome specimen."

Buzz had seen a huge white hand reach out to him, and looking up, he almost wet his pants right there. Standing above him was a face that was black. He didn't know people could be black, so assumed this was not a person but a creature with a black face and white hands, and his father was telling this creature to take him away. "Go with Giles, and behave," his father had said, and disappeared up some stairs.

Buzz let the white hand take him and they went down a long hallway. The other white hand opened a big door, and they went into a room as big as the whole downstairs of Buzz's house at home. Then the white hand let him go, and the black creature stood beside the big door with his white hands behind his back. The head of an animal hung on the wall over a fireplace. A huge glass light hung from the ceiling. Trees were inside the room, growing in pots. Buzz looked around him, desperately. He knew he could not hold out much longer, and he didn't know if they had a bathroom. He whimpered and crossed his legs and squeezed as hard as he could. The black creature coughed, and Buzz jerked around to look at him. One white hand was pointing at a tree with red flowers growing on it. Buzz looked back at the creature. The creature pointed again. Buzz understood and gratefully rushed to the tree, pulled down his cotton shorts, and let go. When he was done, the black creature came over, pulled up his shorts for him, and together they stood and watched the puddle soak into the dry soil. The creature winked at him, and Buzz winked back. From that day, Giles became one of Buzz's best friends, and though he saw him very little in the years to come, Buzz mourned his death, truly.

His only other memory of a "men only" trip was one that he wasn't sure was real. He must have been older because the book his father had been reading to him at bedtime, a book about fishing, had a misspelled word—"compleat"—on the cover. His father clapped the book shut one night and announced they would go fishing for the Fourth of July holiday. And though Buzz protested as well as he could, his father insisted they would go. Buzz wanted to stay in Bosky Dells and eat fried chicken and potato salad at the town picnic and watch the fireworks. He was told by his mother, "Do what dear daddy tells you to do." So he went. They drove and drove. When they got to the lake, somewhere, and set up their camp, the water was warm and the fish nonexistent. Just at dusk his father packed up, tossed Buzz in the car along with the poles, lures, lines, and sleeping bags, and began the long, tiresome trip home with no explanation. Disappointed about not getting to sleep in a tent and not catching any fish and missing the picnic and the fireworks, Buzz could not help sniffling a little in the back seat. "Don't cry, my stalwart companion," his father had said. "Stalwart companions do not have runny noses." So Buzz had sat there stifling his sobs and wiping his nose on his father's fishing vest when his father wasn't looking.

Just as it was dark, they came to a small lake with a narrow bridge crossing one end of it. There was no town Buzz could recall, but all along the bridge and the road and the lake were cars and people. Buzz's father stopped and leaned out the window. "My good man," he said to someone standing there, "can you tell me what is going on?" "Fireworks," said someone. "You can park down there if you want. Just about to begin."

"Please?" Buzz begged, "Please? I love fireworks."

His father had sighed, but had parked, and from the car windows Buzz had watched the most spectacular and longest display of fireworks he was ever to witness, before or since. When it was over and they left, Buzz curled up on the back seat and slept all the way home.

Years later, when he asked his father if he remembered the Fourth of July when they watched the fireworks off the bridge, his father had looked at him strangely and said, "No, nothing like that in my memory bank." Buzz was confused about it for a long time until he told Willi Rainwater about it. Willi listened to the whole story. He and Willi were fishing, had eaten their catch, were sitting around their little fire. Willi was poking the fire into sparks. Willi said, "Well, either it did happen and your father plumb forgot about it. Or it was a vision. Either way, it doesn't matter. You still saw it. Must be the Indian in you. White folks, pure white folks I mean, don't have visions, well maybe your Catholic sometimes, and people think they're crazy and ought to be locked up if they tell about it." Buzz decided Willi was right, and wasn't perplexed about it any more.

When his father died, Buzz was fourteen, in high school, already in love with the new girl, Glinda True. Buzz wasn't too sad about his father's death, and the body was taken to New Jersey to be buried and everyone in town seemed to forget pretty fast. Two years later, Buzz's mother got married again, this time to a local boy, and, as if to even some old score, he was ten years younger than she was. More like a big brother to Buzz than a stepfather, which was okay, and they got along all right until this guy got a job somewhere else and he and Buzz's mother moved south to Portsmouth. Buzz guessed he was around seventeen or eighteen when that happened. His mother gave him the house and told him to keep the furniture and stuff too, and wrote to him a couple times a year and called on his birthday and sometimes sent money. She was alive and still married and seemed okay from what he could make out, and that was enough for Buzz where she was concerned.

Probably the biggest event in his life was when Glinda True came to town and he was smitten at once by her curly blond hair, her big laugh, and her exciting fun ideas. She played around with him like she did with all the boys, but he had hopes that someday soon she'd settle down and date him steady and someday they'd get married. That was the thing you did in Bosky Dells. You went steady, you graduated, you got a job, you settled down, you got married. For years, she'd go out with him, but she was always going out with lots of guys, some of them from neighboring towns.

She let Buzz get to third base, then almost to homeplate, and she kept telling him there was really no one else. He believed her because he wanted to, not because he thought she was telling the truth. Then she started hanging around with the German man, Buzz thought. One night, he was sure, walking home late from a yard job, he saw them parked way down on the cemetery road. Another time, he saw Glinda go into the man's house without knocking first. He didn't mention this to anybody, and it scared him a little to think of Glinda getting involved, or just walking into a man's house. Then he was pretty sure that the ring with the green jewel in it might have been a present from that man, even though Glinda laughed and told everybody she'd bought it for herself with her savings from the beauty parlor where she now worked. Buzz didn't see how that could be possible. It looked too expensive to him. High school was over now, and both had jobs—Buzz at the dump. Glinda still laughed and joked with him, and sometimes went to the drive-in with him, but she never seemed to take him seriously anymore. But Buzz took life more seriously than he ever had.

Then, all of a sudden, she left town. Though he thought she'd come back after she got tired of the city, she never did. Then there'd been the accident with his truck, Henry Ford, and the moose. Kind of the final straw. Buzz swore he never wanted anything in his life again that mattered to him at all. He wouldn't even have gotten Dog if Puck Diddles hadn't found the poor thing struggling to swim out of the lake with a rock tied around its neck. Puck was going to take him to the pound, but decided a dog watching the dump wouldn't be a bad idea, and Buzz had taken pity on the poor mutt, and so, in a detached way, Dog had come to belong to Buzz. They both took care of themselves most of the time, and of each other once in awhile, and it seemed to work out.

Now, speeding north in the early dark, listening to the radio, and licking the cream of the Twinkie from his lips, Buzz thought he might consult Willi about the funeral and Glinda turning up like that and what it all meant. He'd tell Willi that now that Glinda was alive, nobody knew who the body was at all. He might bring up the subject of visions again, and ask Willi how people could have a vision—bring one on, so to speak. Because Buzz felt he needed something to show him in which direction his life lay, and what he should do now that Glinda was back in town. Willi could help him. Buzz might even trade his snakeskin boots for information such as that.

Chapter VII

Glinda

A hunk. He's a hunk. Him and me—we could do anything together. He deserves it. I deserve him. Marc. God, he doesn't
belong in that Christly fitness salon. That's for sure. He's
got the talent. The looks. Body. Ambition. He just needs a break.
What's he get an hour wasting himself working for "Trim 'N Slim
Ltd." anyhow? He just needs a break. With a break, which I am
about to give him, God knows what he could do. When he says
'Glinda, dollface, with a break, God knows what I could do, you
know?' Wow. That's for sure. When he rubs that one hairy finger
up and down my arm so soft and says that and looks up into my
eyes, I mean, he's so sincere, it kills me. Well, I for one believe him.
I believe in him. Well, I know it! That face, those eyes, that talent?
God knows where it could lead to. Well, girl, gotta make some
plans here, fast. Don't want him to get lonely, do we? Gotta get this
over with, get outta this house, this hole, this town one final goddamn time, and now this fucking mess: my own goddamn funeral.
Terrific. Adele could've spent some of those millions for a new
goddamn tub, though. But, I guess I'm glad she didn't. More for
Marc. For Marc and I.)

Glinda lifts one arm up through the lavender bubbles and grabs
the big plastic bottle and squeezes more purple Spring Blossom
foam bath into the water in Adele's old tub. Probably been right in
this same spot since the invention of plumbing, but Adele had never
replaced it. Its lion feet had long ago clawed through the linoleum.
The tiny chrome faucets, worn down to the brass, one for hot, one
for cold, squirt out spastic little streams of water. They leak, and

ancient rust stains bleed down the front of the tub. A heavy chrome
chain holds a chewed-up rubber stopper. The bottom of the tub is
gritty. Clean, but gritty. The rubber daisies, to prevent slipping, are
a little loose. Right now, though she isn't noticing it, the daisies are
making daisy-shaped ridge marks on Glinda's lobster-red behind.
Red, because the water in the tub is chin high, lavender, and as hot
as Glinda can keep it.

The small bathroom, mostly brown, steams like, well, like
Marc's "sauna time, girls!" back at Trim 'N Slim—exercise rooms,
jazzercise classes, hot tubs, tummy-slimmers, tanning and vegetable
juice bar, music, personalized plans. "You tell us what to slim 'n
we'll trim it!" was the catchy ad in the Sunday magazine section.
Glinda thought she'd slim a little, before the cruise. The cruise she
and Tina, her best girlfriend in the claims department, had signed
up for six months ago. Ten days on a holiday boat, with an
Olympic pool right on board. Nightly dances on board. Fabulous
food cooked by trained chefs. No detail overlooked. Stopovers
("shopping galore!") in "exotic ports o' call!" Shuffleboard! God
knows what else. Continuous entertainment!

With one wrinkly red finger Glinda writes MARC in the hot
lavender bubbles. Little did she know that Marc would be waiting
there at Trim 'N Slim that first day, dressed in pale yellow spandex
with a fluffy towel around his neck. "And who are *we*?" he had
asked, looking up from his clipboard. Glinda thought she'd never
forget his saying that: "And who are *we*?" Name: Glinda True.
"French?" Marc asked. "Half," said Glinda, and despite so many
years of little white lies, felt the blood rush into her face. "Age?"
"Thirty-eight." "Health?" "Oh, terrific!" "Goal?" "Well, I've got a
cruise lined up; thought I'd get in shape, you know . . ." "Cruise?
Lucky, *lucky* us! Where to?" "Oh, the usual. Ports o' call, and all
that kind of thing. Just wanna get in my new bikini, I mean, just,
you know, a pound here, an inch there?" "*No problem!*" And Glinda
thought she'd never forget that, either. "You've come to the right
place!" Marc had said. And Glinda thought, you could say that
again.

"Job?" said Marc, looking up through his eyebrows. "Managing consultant," said Glinda, "for a charitable organization. I, actually, well, I don't even take a salary, if you know what I mean." "Ah, good," said Marc, writing, "yes, I know what you mean. Okay! You're all checked in Glinda, now let's get you suited up, and get you started. One hour in *here*! Traci will be in to get you acquainted with the ma*chines*! Massage later? Hot tub? Both? Your choice, Glinda, just let us know what we can do to make you happy, okay? That's our aim!"

Had he winked? Well, no matter, as he had winked so many times since.

She had always hated this rusty tub. Had always hated taking a bath in it. Naturally there was no shower. One bathroom for everybody. She had always hated this bathroom. She had always hated this house. She hated all the smells from the minute she walked in: mothballs, rubber, rust, pickles, bathmats, wood fires, soap powder, kerosene, teeth, pancakes, wet wool, boiling meat, tea bags, Pet Milk. She had not loved her parents, but hated them for dying. She hated her cousin Adele for living, and not dying. She had little feeling for her grandparents one way or another, though she pretended to dote and fawn. They were never taken in, so didn't like her much, either. She hated Adele's goody-two-shoes. She hated Adele's sullen stares, her tidiness, her churchiness, her big "in" with Gram and Gramps, her stupid aim to be "something," her icky thing on the old fart next door, her good grades, her sexlessness.

She hated sharing a room with Adele who, even at seventeen, eighteen, snored a little and wore a hairnet to bed. She soon came to hate the smells of motor oil and barn disinfectant because every boy in town smelled like either or both, and it got on her skin, in her hair, on her clothes. Sometimes she tasted one, or both. She hated boys with wet combed-back hair. She hated school, the books, the teachers, the stuff they got excited about. She got the other students to laugh, and she got them to sneer. The kids in town had laughed before, but sneering was something new. Glinda knew she had power because she was "from away" and was cute and sexy. Soon she taught them to laugh, sneer, and then pout. In detention (for laughing, and then sneering) everyone now pouted, looked murderous, sat with their arms crossed on their chests. These pouting and murderous expressions replaced the former pale, crestfallen, chastised expressions in detention which pleaded: I'm sorry; do my folks have to know about this? In a few months, Glinda taught the faces to say: stick it up your stovepipe.

If Glinda had ever loved anything or anybody but herself, no one had noticed it or felt it and so it never got remembered. Adele remembered the years with Glinda, but whenever she thought about them a curtain of blood or ice fell down over her mind. Buzz remembered Glinda, of course, and the feel of her, her laugh and smell and the sweaters and all, and though he had never received love, he still sometimes felt what he thought would go by that name. Many people in town had never heard of her. Harold Mosby told his baseball card that he remembered what she looked like. Snooky only knew her from Adele's infrequent remarks as "that bizarre cousin of yours," but had never met her. Other folks who did recall her felt a slight chill, or hitch, or withdrawal when her name came up, which wasn't often. At least not until her body turned up at the dump. In the front of their minds, they could still conjure up a kind of cute blond in a too-small fuzzy sweater who had left town quite a while ago, a disturbance of the peace they were well shed of.

Up to the time of her parents' car wreck, Glinda had been raised downstate in a mild, practical sort of way. Her folks had hoped for a boy. But that can't explain anything. Her dad worked in a hardware store, a respectable job. Her mother kept house. Glinda was never abused, never neglected, never deprived. The worst that could be said is that her early life had been colorless. It was responsible, peaceful, comfortable, loving in a mild way, dull meals on time, dull questions: "and what did you learn today, Glinda?" over casserole or canned fruit salad.

Anyone might have hoped for more passion, maybe even some raised voices now and then, loud music, storms, fights, convictions, extremes. Dying in a wrecked and burning Nash, which they'd driven for years, was the only extreme thing her parents ever did.

So nothing can account, in a way, for Glinda's empty badness, her dullness, her hardness of heart, her dull troublemaking. She had been born this way, it seems, and beyond this she never grew. When her parents were killed, she made a great show at school and at the church memorial service and enjoyed the stares, the sympathy, and the notoriety. Then she was moved to Gram and Gramp's house with very little publicity of any kind. Perhaps she had been born without the ability to love anything but herself, and, following that dull birth, a simple and unstimulating home didn't help. Plus she was spoiled, being an only child. Now she is forty-eight or thirty-eight or whatever, and still hates this bathtub as much as she hated it at sixteen. And for exactly the same reasons.

Since she fled Bosky Dells, Glinda has worked for an insurance company in Boston, lived alone (never married) in a series of efficiency apartments, and has never loved even so much as a cat. Years of girlfriends and years of dates. None of it came to much, but then she still thinks of herself as young. The closest she has ever come to glamour was the ten-day cruise with her friend, Tina. Glinda canceled the cruise when she met Marc at the fitness salon. She told Tina something about "doctor's advice" and forfeited the down payment to the travel agent. She told Marc her stockbroker had advised her not to leave the country at this time, given the "iffy" market. Marc said he understood, and that was "just too bad." She said, "Oh well, just a few days in the sun." Marc said, "But I bet you could've used a break." She said, "Oh, not really. Duty first, you know."

In canceling her long-awaited cruise, Glinda shows some wisdom, even though she forfeits her down payment. Because in ten days without her in town, Marc would most certainly have found someone else among his "clients." Another rich (as he believes) man-hungry old maid (as he thinks) who would, bluntly put, buy him things. Big things.

Marc believes that in exchange for their money and coddlings, he repays women handsomely, probably better than they deserve. With glances, purrs, struttings, winks, fussy concerns about their health and diet, picturesque sulks, tucking-ups at night, clucks, occasional cheap bouquets bought from pushcarts, muscles to look at or touch, little reprimands, repeated tellings of his life story and, mainly, his needs. His needs (which he prefers to think of as their need to be needed) are to be coddled, admired, exclaimed over, fondled just a little, lavished with expensive presents, and otherwise left strictly alone. In this sense, Marc is a simple man. If he has one firm belief, it is that women, like Glinda, want to "mother" him, whether they know it or not. So he lets them. They do so, thinking of it as "foreplay."

If he has sexual feelings, they are weak and intermittent, and are felt for Traci the exercise instructor, and others of her age, build, muscle tone, aspirations, and wardrobe. These feelings are mostly in his mind. In fact, they are entirely in his mind. Certainly Marc is not so beset by sexual desire as his handsome face, body, spandex, voice, purrs, noodlings, winks, cologne, and repeated storytellings apparently lead Glinda and other women to believe. The fantasy of owning a Rolex, a silk suit, a monogrammed cocktail shaker, or going on a cruise—these things are the main event to Marc. Sex is the preliminary, or the setting, as it were, in which a Rolex might happen.

Naturally, to sane women (and Glinda is sane in this conventional way), the watch, suit, and cruise would be seen as the setting, with the main event—love—to follow. However, because Marc and any woman he's letting mother him are both lying about so many things, both play their hands very carefully and thus try never to understand each other at all. This, of course, is in their best interests.

In this way, the affair between Marc and anyone, Glinda included, could not be said to "progress," but it could be said that it had "arrived," almost at first glance, at a mutually convenient standstill. Marc has now "had" many of these affairs which he, never the woman, brings to an end with a long (sometimes it takes him months) plea about "finding himself," "loving" her, but "needing time." The women eventually let him go, shamed into looking desperate.

But now he, too, is losing his looks, a little. His grasp—well, he has never given much thought to that. He is also older than he says he is, his black hair gets a touch-up now and then. He has nowhere to go, and no further act up his sleeve. If Glinda got stuck at hate, he got stuck at cute. Both he and Glinda know that each other is thinking their "love" is some kind of last chance. Neither one says they feel this way. Neither says they know the other feels it. He knows Glinda is older than she claims, but thinks she is older than she really is. Glinda thinks Marc is ready to settle down.

Though he does not know it yet, it is for Marc than Glinda has bought the red convertible and has returned to Bosky Dells and to this hated bathtub, this hated house, and hateful Adele. To trudge back to this hole for one clear purpose and then accidentally walk in on her own funeral was about as much typical hicky confusion and fuck up as Glinda could stand. Therefore she is taking this long, lavender, and very hot bath in order to think.

If Adele, downstairs in her old man's bathrobe and fuming over the waste of water overhead, had known any of the above story, or that someone spelled Marc with a "c," she would not have believed it. Even if someone trusted, like Snooky, were to tell her, face to face and with supporting evidence, she would not believe it. It does not make a lot of difference, at this point in her life, whether or not Glinda believes it, either. Because hell, high water, or horse manure, it is for this story and for Marc that she is here, in this tub, in these bubbles, in this mess, in this house. At least for a few more days.

There is quite a bit of money involved in this plot. True to Yankee custom, however, little of it has been spent on anything for a long, long time. Not even on new rubber nonslip daisies for the tub bottom. No one would even guess all that money exists.

However, because of on-the-job training in computers, and a sudden curiosity, and a few chums in other helpful offices here and there, Glinda now knows exactly what it comes to and which bank is taking care of it.

Chapter VIII

In Which Harold Confesses
And Is Absolved

Harold stood in the yard of the Rectory and sniffed the supper smells wafting through the open kitchen window. Open because it was another warm day for November, but mainly because Snooky had burned some garlic. Harold had a very keen nose and never forgot something he had smelled, so he knew Snooky was cooking Chicken Marbella. One of Harold's favorites. Asparagus tips on the side, like last time? And was that the steamy scent of a blackberry pie? Snooky was banging pans and singing the toreador song. He must have been reading his book on Spain again, Harold decided. Snooky had read the book to Harold twice now. It was called *Spain*. Harold thought the book was okay and would have been glad to listen to it again, as long as Snooky kept a steady supply of scones and finger rolls available, which Harold called (in his mind) "biscuits" and "little hot dog buns with stuff inside."

"Up to another chapter, Old Boy?" Snooky would ask. "Oh dear, out of snackeroos. Let me hustle out and get some more. Sit patient, and we'll read on."

Harold would nod and Snooky would mark their page with his red bookmark, lay the book carefully on the seat of the green Morris chair, and go out to the kitchen. Presently he would return with another plate of good little things, set them on the low table next to Harold's stool, and begin to read again. Harold would sit agreeably while Snooky read on, with lots of expression, about people called Barcelona and Seville and a group known as the Gauls. Harold figured, in the course of two readings, he had eaten about five hundred little hot dog buns stuffed with things. All very delicious.

Today Harold knew there would be no bullfights, no matadors, no Gauls, no sunny hillsides, no biscuits. It was obvious that Snooky was in a cooking mood. Still, if Harold hung around, he might get asked to supper. Or maybe it was still early enough for leftovers from lunch. He rapped gently on the door. At the same moment, he heard the thumping of Father's walker coming down the hall to the kitchen. Snooky stopped singing and Harold heard a pan getting slammed into the sink.

"*How* am I to do everything? Cook. Clean. Be doorman. Yes, I'm coming. Oh, come in, for heaven's sake."

Harold almost left. But the smells of chicken and the pie held him. He rapped again.

Snooky appeared at the door, his hair puffing from the sides of his head, his face red, his apron smeary and wrinkled.

"Oh, Harold, it's you. Well, I can't stop to talk now, I'm halfway through something with Julia." Harold's heart sank and he turned to go. "Oh well, wait," said Snooky. "Come on in. I'll tell you what, Harold, would you do me a huge, huge favor?" Harold nodded. Snooky resumed, "It *is* such a nice afternoon. What if I take the Old Holy out to the porch and you entertain him till dins? Would you like that, Padre? *Like* that! The porch! Harold wants to visit you a while! *Yes*, I'll bring him some tea or something. Tea or something! Oh, Harold, you have *no* idea. Well, off you go and I'll get him a sweater and bring him out in a minute."

Harold went out to the porch and sat down on the steps. The porch faced west; the sunshine was warm. Today seemed more like September than almost mid-November. A late Indian summer breeze shook the last of the leaves from the two big birches, and Harold watched them float down to the brown grass on the lawn. Some geese flew overhead. You couldn't fool geese, Harold thought, smiling. These would be trailers, the last to leave the lake for warmer climes. Gosh, Spain, maybe. Harold had lived in Bosky Dells his whole life; maybe longer, he thought to himself. So he knew it could snow tomorrow. He smiled again. You can't fool geese and you can't fool Harold P. Mosby, either, not when it comes to weather.

He leaned back against the rail. This old porch held lots of memories for him. That was the best thing about porches. Porches were great memory places. A lot of living took place on them, and sometimes dying, too. At least three or four people Harold could recall had died sitting on their porches. Just slipped away nodding in their Boston rockers. Like Miss Look, the librarian there, her grandmother. She sat down one summer night and died on the porch while she knitted and purled on an afghan for the Church Fair. Of course, she was ninety-seven at the time; still, she died unexpectedly. At least, she didn't expect it because if she had, she probably would have started on a smaller project. And then there was Puck's Uncle Clyde. Was that house down the street? Or was it out at the farm? Anyhow, Uncle Clyde went out to drink his coffee on the stoop one morning and died right there. He wasn't known for being too ambitious, so no one noticed anything unusual until he didn't come in for dinner. The doctor said he'd probably passed on sometime long before noon though, judging by how cold he was by the time they did try to find him.

Harold thought about this porch. He had spent many hours as a kid sitting on this porch. That was when the house had belonged to Mr. Kringle and a long long long time before Father and Snooky had moved in. And before Mr. Kringle had died like he did. Harold frowned. Ever since the big funeral a few weeks ago, he had, off and on, been overwhelmed with emotion. A kind of sick feeling in his stomach that made him think he might be hungry but really wasn't.

Harold desperately wished he could make words come out. They were all there, inside his head; they just wouldn't come out. Or maybe they wouldn't come out right and people would laugh and laugh. If he could speak, he could go to the police. Or he could go to the minister at the church. He could have told his mother; course she was dead. Honus understood, but Harold wished Honus could say that to him, exactly those words. "It's okay, Harold," he wished the baseball card could say. But Honus really couldn't. Talk back. Harold really knew that. But he'd like to tell somebody and get all this bad feeling out of his stomach. He would tell them about Mr. Kringle, and the gun, and the banister, and about his baseball card coming home.

Harold could hear Snooky bringing Father down the hall.

"Yes, you *do* want to sit out awhile. It's just lovely out there. No, it isn't suppertime. Not for two hours. Besides, Harold needs your company. Isn't that nice? NICE! Of course you like Harold. You're a priest. You like *everyone*!"

Harold heard the thump-thump as Snooky guided Father to the door.

"Here he is!" Snooky sang out. "Now you two boys have a nice chat and I'll get back to work. Tea, any minute. YES, something with it. Harold, you're a dear."

Father Kildare pushed the screen door with the walker, thumped onto the porch, and sank into the big rocker. Snooky fussed around him, arranging a red, green, and yellow afghan over his knees.

"There! All cozy," he declared. "He's being a bit vague today, Harold. He's been reading all morning which is not good for him, and quoting somebody or other every time I ask him something, which is *not* good for me. I mean at one point I said to him, 'Ready for lunch?' And he said something like 'I greet you at the beginning of a great career.' And I said 'Well, do tell! I've only been slaving over your food for forty years now, I'd hardly call it the beginning!' Anyway, do what you can. I'm sure you'll think of something to talk about. Well, you know what I mean," and with that, Snooky disappeared down the hall.

Harold turned his attention to Father Kildare who was drumming his fingers in an odd little beat of his own on the arms of his chair. A fly circled his face and he flapped his hand at it. He grunted and closed his eyes, letting the sun shine on his wrinkled lids. Harold watched him.

If only I could speak, he was thinking. Father wasn't a Catholic, but he was a Father, and a Father was a Father, wasn't he? Harold felt his burden rumble in his stomach again, and he groaned. I want to talk to him, Harold thought. I want to tell him. I want to tell him what I did. What I did to Mr. Kringle, but I didn't mean it.

"'No man has ever stated his griefs as lightly as he might,'" said Father Kildare.

Harold stared in disbelief and played the words over in his head like a record. Just to be sure he understood. Could it be? Was it possible? This surely was the work of the Almighty, Catholic or not. Father Kildare was actually hearing his thoughts.

"'Either God is there or not,'" said Father, flatly.

Harold was delirious with joy. His thoughts went fast and bumped into each other, so eager they were to be spoken.

"Father," Harold thought on, "Father, years ago I did an awful thing. It was so awful that I've never told anyone about it. But now I want to tell you."

"'Believe and love,'" said the old priest, "'A believing love will relieve us of a vast load of care.'"

Harold was beside himself. He rushed on.

"I *do* have a vast load of care," he thought, "but you see, Father, I have this baseball card. My father gave it to me when I was little. And he told me if I was ever in need I should show it to somebody with money. One night I was really hungry and needed some supper really bad so I knew Mr. Kringle had money and I took the card to show it to him. And I did and Mr. Kringle didn't give me anything to eat or nothing but he gave me back my card and he said it was worth thousands. I don't know how he knew that, but that's what he said."

"'Each man has his own vocation. The talent is the call.'" said Father.

"Well," Harold rushed on in his head, "one day my card was missing. I always keep it right where I know it is and it was gone. And I knew Mr. Kringle had to have it on account've nobody else knew about it. So I waited till dark and then I went to his house to get it back. You see, Father, Mr. Kringle and me, we knew each other pretty well. Sometimes I stacked wood for him, or he'd have me get his groceries or his letters, things like that. He didn't like to go out too much, you know."

"'He shall have his own society,'" said Father Kildare. Harold pondered the wonder of it for a moment.

"That's just it, Father! His own society. Plus me, sometimes. Well, sometimes there was a woman there, too. I mean, besides

Miss Adele and Miss Glinda. This woman was different than them. A lot different, if you know what I mean. Taller. Well, different. Anyway," his thoughts went forward, "the night I went there for my card she wasn't there and neither was no one else. Mr. Kringle was all alone. So, I snuck in through a open window to try and find Honus. I was looking in all the drawers and then I accidental knocked something off the desk. I was some scared, I can tell you that, Father. And then Mr. Kringle heard me and he came after me with a gun, he didn't know it was me on account've I had my cap pulled way down, you know, like in the movies? And by then I was upstairs and he came running up the stairs and he was waving his gun and it scared me and I pushed him, I pushed him real hard, and he fell down the stairs and hit the banister and I think the gun went off and he was hurt, bad. And then I ran down the stairs and I was going to go back out the window and he crawled after me and he was crying and I crawled out the window and he just went to sleep on the floor because I looked back in and then they found him. But he didn't mean to shoot me and I didn't mean to shoot him but it was my fault. I killed him but I didn't mean to do it and I don't know what to do, I just want to be forgiven."

"'Never was a sincere word utterly lost,'" Father Kildare said, his eyes closed.

"Oh Father, this is the truth. And then, then, when I check on Honus a couple days later, he was there all right, wrapped in his blanket. I don't know how he got there, but he was there. See, Father, I always wanted to tell somebody but I didn't know how to do it."

Father Kildare was silent for a long time. He rocked, with his eyes shut. Harold knew he was thinking hard. From inside the house came the clatter of dishes and Snooky singing. Another V of geese went overhead. The afternoon air smelled like tomatoes cooking but it also smelled like snow. Harold couldn't figure that out. Must be an odd time of year, he thought. Always had been.

Father Kildare spoke. "'When a man speaks the truth in the spirit of the truth,'" he said, placing his gnarled hand on Harold's shoulder, "'his eye is as clear as the heavens.'" The fly buzzed in front of Father's face as he said those words. He raised his hand and waved it once in front of his eyes, raised it to shoo the fly from his forehead, and then let it drop slowly into his lap again.

Harold stared at him. The sign of forgiveness, he remembered that from church so long ago. Father had heard. And he, Harold, was forgiven. He was free. Forgetting all about chicken and black-berry pie and asparagus tips, he got to his feet and skipped across the lawn. He must tell Honus about this great miracle, whatever Honus had to say about it. With his heart roaring and with a smile behind his lips, Harold raced home to his car.

Quite a while after he had left, Father Kildare opened his eyes and said, "And Harold, don't forget, 'We know the secret of the world is profound, but who or what shall be our interpreter, we know not,'" and with that, he drifted off to sleep, murmuring be-tween snores. In the kitchen, the Chicken Marbella stewed in its sauce and Snooky had his head in the refrigerator, looking for some little thing for tea. To the ragged opening bars of the toreador song, he sang an unconscious fragment of the day: "The uh-uh sun is but a morn-ing star, the uh-uh sun is butta morn-ing star," and began again.

Chapter IX

In Which the Town Gets Ready
For Thanksgiving and Glinda Has a Visitor

It's now the Wednesday before Thanksgiving Day which is early this year. Clyde tells the other coffee drinkers at the Store that's on account of daylight savings and "messin' around with time all the time." The others in the booth—Gerald, Milton who holds the plowing contract, Clyde's second cousin Moose, and Harold (who is standing)—don't think this theory sounds right, but they all nod anyhow as though Clyde had made a decisive point. They don't want to get into it with him right now because they want to stick to the subjects they've kept warm all morning, which are: "what the hell is takin' the police this long to figure out who got murdered at the dump?" and "so when can we expect to get back to normal around here?"

Though at noon on this cold overcast day which promises snow or at least freezing rain before it is done, things in downtown Bosky Dells seem normal enough. The coffee crowd waxed, waned, and now it's the lunch crowd. Puck came in and stood around for a while, looked at his watch, and left in a hurry. Across from the Store at the Grange Hall, the local crafts people are sweeping up scraps of orange-and-black crepe paper, brown apple cores, and candy wrappers left from the preschoolers' Hallowe'en Party, and dragging in boughs to decorate for the Early Bird Pre-Christmas Craft Fair on Saturday. Two trucks loaded with lashed-down Scotch pines just gassed up and are headed south to Boston's Xmas Tree Mart. ("Talk about easy money," says someone around the coffee pot.) Adele, sick of staying at home and waiting—for what, she doesn't know—is putting tinsel wreaths in the two front windows of About Thyme and blowing on her fingers as she tapes WINTER HOURS—TUE. THRU SAT., 11 TO 2, on the front door.

Up next to the cash register in the Store, a clipping of a few weeks back from the state's largest daily reads: "Hallowe'en Prank Carried Too Far? Body Found in Hamlet's Transfer Stati . . . " and part of the story is covered up by the running tally of bucks, does, weights, and name of the hunter if local.

The day is so dark already that the automatic timer has turned on the blinking Christmas lights thumbtacked around the Store's plate-glass window. Over the past weekend, the two clerks took their Sunday afternoon to turn the big plate-glass window into small "panes" with strips of masking tape. Onto the bottom of each "pane" they squirted a little aerosol "snow." Real snow, shoved by the plow against the front of the Store, nearly obliterates the bottom two rows of "frosted" panes. It looks very festive, though, and everyone enjoys it.

Outside in the parking lot, next to the two gas tanks, the portable signboard had read SHOP NOW—EARLY CLOSING THANKSGIVING A.M.. However, at some point during the past week, someone (the teen-agers?) had rearranged the movable letters so that the sign now reads GIVING AWAY HAMS. No one has noticed this.

The noon school bus has just dropped the village kinder-gartners in front of the Store. Mothers, a few fathers, a few grand-parents, are waiting, engines idling. Dwarf Indians in construction paper headdresses and dwarf Pilgrims in black cardboard hats jump from the last bus step, run to their respective cars and pick-ups, and struggle with door handles, lunch boxes, knitted caps, mittens, crumpled artwork of smiling turkeys, lined tablet paper with rows of a a a a a a a a and m m m m m.

Inside the Store, Snooky is rummaging through the canned mushrooms trying to find caps or whole instead of stems and pieces, and casting dark despairing glances upward at the buzzing neons in the ceiling. Little Timmy Noble (a distant cousin to Buzz) stands in his headdress with his runny nose on the edge of the checkout counter and sings in a high thin voice to no one in particular—

> Five fat turkeys are wee-eee,
> Spent the night in a tree-eee,
> The cook came round
> We couldn't be found
> That's why we're here you see-eee . . .

And his mother hisses, "Cut it out, I'm tellin' you, or you're gonna get whacked upside the head and wait in the Christly truck, you hear me?" He pouches out his cheeks and stares blankly ahead of him at the midriff of the checkout clerk, who says, "He's some growed on us this year, I guess," to which his mother nods grimly and asks for one package of generic menthol lites.

"Well," says Gerald, leaning into the booth, "'Look,' I tode him, I says, 'Can we get this goddamn thing settled here pretty soon?' And he goes, 'The in-ves-tee-ga-shun la-di-da is proceeding as smooth as possible.' And I go, 'Well, let's get this thing on the road here on accounta it's keepin' everybody so danged upset and wooly.' And he goes, 'Patience my good man,' or some such fuckin' thing like that, 'this sort of thing takes time,' and I go, 'Yeah, don't it though.'"

"Yeah," says Clyde. "Our tax dollars, too."

"Not eggsakly," says Milton, peering through the fake snow to see if the real snow has started. "That cop, that Sergeant, how you say his name? is a Mass. cop, not local. Not our taxes, if I'm thinkin' straight on this issue."

"Well, it is too! I mean, he's workin' now for our police, ain't he? So, what's that costin' us? I mean, Mass. ain't payin' him to look into some diddly-shit, half-assed murder up here, are they?"

"Int his name same as the bassetball team? the Selts?"

"All I can say is what he tells me—'they are lookin' into it.'"

"Pass that Cremora down here, wouldja? Well, not the way I'd do things."

"Or they useta be, I'll guaranfuckintee you that."

"Not by a long shot."

"Who called him in the first place?"

"Jesus, Clyde, give it a rest, will ya? Nobody called him. How many times you gotta be told that? He just fuckin' turned up like, accidental," says Gerald, who is tired. "Now he wants me to take him up Gaffer Mountain for a day of sittin' on my ass in the ass-freezin' cold waitin' for his deer to walk up and say 'shoot me, please, good sir,' and I'll be damned if I think this is gettin' us anyplace here."

"Are they keepin' her cold all this time?"

"Well, of course not. Think about it, would you, for five minutes? Whatted be the point? That'd be pretty ignorant, wouldn't it? No meat on her, is there?"

"How do they know it's a her?"

"Don't know. They can just tell stuff like that, I think."

"Who's payin' the bill for all this, that's what I wanna know. Us, or the State?"

"I still say the kids did it."

"Yeah, and how . . . oh screw it," said Gerald, "what's the point."

"Well, they could've!"

"And you tell me where they'd've got the body, okay? You tell me that, and you win the lottery, too. Megabucks. Well, so he goes, 'If not this Miss Glinda True person, then who could it be, do you suppose?' And I go, 'Look, Celted, you're the expert. Haven't we been over this about one million Christly times? Look, if I were you,' I say, 'I'd go on back home and forget the whole thing. I mean, it's got've been a long time ago, right? Let's let what's gone by stay there. Far as I know,' I tode him, 'nobody's been missin' around here for as long as I can think, and I just think this whole goddamn thing is better kep' down and closed up now. Has anybody come forward?' I says? And he goes, 'Isn't that the point?' And I go, 'So? I don't get it.' And he says, 'Let's review this once more. Who was familiar with this Miss Glinda True . . .'"

"Who wasn't, more like." (Laughter all around the booth, but hushed.)

"So I tode him, 'The trail is cold, isn't it? We're just pissin' in the wind here,' I said. 'Let what's gone by stay that way for once.'"

"Well, I'm not so sure folks appreciate his pokin' his nose into our town affairs anyhow. I don't see why we needed to call in an outta state cop. I think we can take care of our own business if push comes to pull around here."

"Shove."

"What?"

"Shove, not pull."

"Well. Whatever. I still say those kids did it."

"Right, Clyde. When they ain't doin' God knows what drugs, drunk on their ass, smashin' their daddy's trucks and diddlin' their cousins, they just go round the countryside diggin' up whole entire skeletons and puttin' jewels on their fingers and then hidin' 'em in the dump in case Harold here decides to go treasure hunting. Just for the pure hell of it."

"And who ordered the burger here? Chowda? Turkey Delight? Sausage pizza? Dog with the works? All on one?" says the waitress, Ginny, to the assembled table. "And how's Snooky today?" to Snooky who pats by in his slippers and gives her a black look. "And how's Gerald today, okay Gerald? How's that investigation doin'? Caught anybody yet? Everybody all set? Sorry, Clyde, outta slaw today, sorry about that."

"Okay, Ginny," says Gerald. "I mean, I'm okay and we're all set here, and about the investigation, all I am at liberty to say at this time is that they are lookin' into it."

The waitress nods, is making out five separate lunch checks. "Just what they say on the TV," she says, "so I guess they are. I mean, lookin' into it."

Adele slips in the back way, hoping to avoid the sight of Glinda in her "leisure suit," whatever that might be for. Hoping to avoid the rattle of the noontime TV talk show in the front room. Hoping to make herself a solitary cup of tea, a solitary sandwich of cold baked beans. Quietly, she shuts the kitchen door behind her, quietly eases shut the door into the hallway, when she hears the front door buzzer and then Glinda curse from somewhere in the house, and then footsteps. Adele presses her good ear against the panel of the hallway door and holds her finger to her lips and looks a warning at Fido. "Oh, Snooky," thinks Adele, "please don't call me right now, all right?"

Glinda's perky "Why hello there!" And a deep grumble in reply. The front door shuts. Footsteps going into the front room. The TV turned off. Glinda's squeaky voice. Squeak, rumble, squeak. This is no good, thinks Adele, and carefully holding one hand against the panels, she inches the hall door open a crack and hears Glinda saying "I know what you mean! I'm leaving as soon as I can, too! What's there for a city-lover like me to do in a place like this if you know what I mean!" Rumble. Rumble. Celted? "Winter *soon*!" Glinda shrieks, "Tell me about it! I only meant a few days' visit, you know. Would've left ages ago if you, you big bad man, had let me go!" Adele opens the crack a little wider.

"I believe," rumble, rumble, "I am convinced," (Yes, that Sergeant Celted!) "that can be any day now. Just—any—day—now. And, will you return to your home in Boston?" (Why does he speak so slowly? Is he writing everything he says himself down in his little notebook?)

"Oh, God yes, as soon as possible. Yes. And, Adele is going with me. Did I tell you that before? Yes, she needs a break from all this, don't you think? Poor old thing. She's going back with me for at least the holidays, see some bright lights, do some shopping. Well, just between you and I, I'm trying to convince her to sell this place and move in with me permanent like, you know?"

Another long silence. Would he be writing all that down? That bundle of lies? A trip to Boston. First time Adele had heard that plan. Plan my eye. Could Glinda be serious? Could she actually want her to come for a visit? No, of course not. Watch out for traps. This is some typical wickedness, the usual pack of lies, something to make Glinda look nice to this man, this detective person. Oh, Glinda, you don't fool me, though.

"There are—just—a—few details I'd , um, like to go through— again. I know we've discussed this down at headquarters several times, but—for the official report—and believe me, we are getting very close now—just review for me—one more time if you would—just how you think your purse and your identification papers and of course your—watch? no, ring, wasn't it—came to be with the remains?"

Adele listens to Glinda clear her throat. "Well, look, like I told you before," she begins, "now, to the best I can recall, well, I hope I can remember one more time. Do we really need to go through all this again? Well. I was about to leave town, had, I mean, this is such a long time ago, well, I was all ready to leave and my purse, well, it just turned up missing. Of course I thought it had been stolen. My ring was in my purse. I was, well, yes, I'd gone to the dance, right? Told you that before, didn't I? Yes, night before I was supposed to leave, I went to this dance, a little like a farewell party, you could say. Oh, with a crowd. No one in particular. In fact, like I told you, didn't I? the kids I was with, they're all gone by now, not a one left that I can think of. Another reason I can't stand this place, all my friends knew enough to get out, too. Where was I? Oh yeah, and then, like I think I told you before, it was stolen off our table, ring and all. That's the last I saw of it. I mean, until the other day. And so Adele was kind enough to help me out with the price of a new bus ticket and all. And, I caught that bus, I'm sure of it, that I was getting anyhow. I just figured at the time some punk, you know? Anything else?"

"And the ring?"

"Sergeant, believe it or not, but I have had my admirers! I told you where I got that ring—Mr. Kringle. Well of course he was much too old for me, but he had such a thing on me, you know? And being so rich and all, he gave everybody these gorgeous presents—well not quite as gorgeous as my ring unless you want to count that truck—which I must say, my ring, I mean, I'm glad to have returned at last, though it is a little weird wearing it, let me say that. Anything else?"

"And when you left, you never saw him again?"

"No! Like I told you before, I've never been back at all! I mean, I've always intended to get back, and so here I am at last. But I mean, once I got down to Boston and got such a good job and all, why time just flew I guess. I didn't—like—owe him anything. No, never saw him again or heard. Didn't expect to. Then, too too sad, I was really broken up about it, he killed himself right after I left, and I'm sure it wasn't over me, but I did have some bad moments when I heard about it. I'm sure in a way he couldn't get over me leaving, poor old thing. Anything else?"

"My understanding is that he—killed himself—within a day or two of your having moved away?"

"Oh, that's right. That's right. I mean, that's all I can recall. Well, all these details. But that sounds right, now that I think about it."

"But my understanding is that he killed himself—within a day or two?"

"Well, that could be. Yes, that sounds right. What I meant was, when I heard about it, I felt real bad."

"When would that have been? That you heard about it?"

"Jesus Christ. Sorry about that. It's just too long ago, honestly, I can't remember all this stuff, which day this, which day that. I mean I've tried to be as much help as I can and if you think this has all been easy, my own funeral and all, then your head is up your . . . Look, anything else? I mean, I'd be glad to help you with anything else, but you just can't expect me to remember every little thing."

"Right. And how, I've forgotten, how . . . or rather, did you have a theory about how your purse and watch, ring—sorry—ring, could have turned up with the victim?"

"Now, look, Sergeant, you're an intelligent person, I can tell. Like I told you before, all I can figure is that the corpse stole it. I mean, of course, before it was one. Look, this is really getting to me. Like I told you before, I have no idea, zero, none. It'd be different if I could see what the body looked like, well, you know what I mean. That might be somebody who was at the dance, like somebody we knew from outta town or something. It's not like I can tell who it is any more, is it? I just figure what might've happened is somebody—the corpse—stole my purse at the dance, with my ring in it, and then got lost going home, drunk or something, wandered into the dump. And just stayed there all this time. You know, just somehow got buried up? What else could it have been? That's actually my best shot, you know. Sad. Terribly sad. But what can you do. Anything else?"

"There may be—one or two—details later, but yes—that's all for now and thanks again for your cooperation. It has been a great, yes, help."

"Hey, no problem. And no hard feelings. Look, let's get together once we get back to civilization, okay? When all this blows over? Maybe during the holidays, a little nog or something? I gave you my number, didn't I?"

Footsteps. Rumble. Squeak. Laughter. Front door opens. Rumble. Door shuts. Lies, lies, and more lies, thought Adele, finally taking a breath and easing shut the hallway door. Lies, lies, lies, from beginning to end. Then again, a good thing, I guess. Under the circumstances.

Chapter X

In Which Harold Mosby Plays Detective

As Harold headed back to his car in the fading November afternoon, the snow that had been promised all day, both by the sky and the weather wizards down at the Store, was just beginning to fall. Harold was glad he had a snug car and a warm Purple Haze to go home to, and he couldn't help but feel a little extra-exuberant as he caught the thin flakes on his stuck-out tongue.

The snow would make everyone in town feel real happy, he knew. Most especially happy would be the deer hunters, who with just a few days left to bag their first (or second, or even third) deer, would be out early next morning, even though it was Thanksgiving Day, looking for hoofprints in the fresh snow. The snow would also add some meaning to the rehearsals for the Christmas Pageant down at the Hall. Everyone would begin to feel very Christmasy, and someone would begin to hum a festive song, and someone else would join in, and pretty soon the whole big room would sound like a beehive on fire. And while Harold could not sing, he could hum, so he could join right in with the rest of them. His favorite carol was "'Tis the Gift to Be Simple," and while it wasn't strictly a holiday song, once the entire seasonal repertoire had been gone through a few times, someone would be sure to buzz in with it, sooner or later.

Harold knew Snooky would also be inspired by the snow and would go through all the boxes in the attic of the Rectory until he found his English cookie cutters in the shapes of pears, chickens, robins, red roe bucks (he told Harold), and crowns with HRH on them, and a thin looking Santa Claus. Then, in a baking fit, Snooky would make dozens of cookies all with silver sprinkles on them or colored sugar. He would then pack them in a shoe box and bring them down to the Hall during rehearsal. Everyone would praise the cookies and say he was a "real gourmet cook." Snooky would shuffle and turn red as an apple and say, "Lord, nothing at all, good people, nothing at all," and then stay up all night making some more.

Even Puck, who was Santa this year, seemed to get into the spirit of the thing, and would insist on driving anyone home who did not have a ride. Harold always took him up on the offer, even though he lived only a block past the Hall, because he greatly admired BRNSGR, if not Puck himself, and this year was hoping that he might even get a ride in the new pink car, CTNCND.

As happy as he was, Harold was a little disconcerted by all the talk at the Store today. Everyone was getting very sick and tired of the whole murder, and Harold sensed that if it were not for this Boston policeman, Mr. Celted, that the whole murder thing would have died a natural death a long time ago. Also, it didn't sound like Mr. Celted was doing a very good job. "Leave it to a flatlander in a uniform to keep things stirred up and ballsed up," said Puck at the store just this afternoon. The folks from Patchouli & All were standing around waiting for the UPS delivery man, and even they had taken an uncharacteristic stand. That is, uncharacteristic of them to take a stand, but they had said it was time to "put all this behind us and get on with our lives." Harold felt he had to agree with that. After all, how could the town concentrate on Christmas when there was all this turmoil about a dead body? Harold loved Christmas.

The only two books Harold had ever read cover to cover were both mysteries. Of course he'd heard *Spain*, but that was not a mystery story as far as he could tell, and anyhow it's not the same as reading to yourself. Of the two books he'd read by himself, one was called *Cherry Ames, Girl Detective*, and the other was *The Hardy Boys and The Secret Cave*. Harold preferred Cherry to the Hardy boys, but for appearance's sake, he envisioned himself as Harold Mosby, Boy Detective. Only really, he meant Harold Mosby, Man

Detective. No matter; as he trotted homeward in the falling snow, he was devising a plan to solve this murder mystery better than the policeman had done and get Bosky Dells on the Christmas track.

To solve a mystery, Harold knew the first thing you had to have were clues. And Harold knew where to look. In the back of his car was an old cardboard box, and in this box were various assorted articles that Harold had bought as a grab bag at the auction held at Mr. Kringle's house after his sad funeral. When no heirs to his rightful possessions could be located, the town took control of the situation at last and disposed of the house and belongings in the auction tradition. Everything went to the highest bidder, and if there was no bidder, then it went to anyone who wanted it. This was how Harold stood around that day and finally came by the box.

Down at the Store this afternoon, Harold had heard Puck say to the UPS delivery man, "Betcha that old German was tied in with this somehow, betcha anything." And the UPS man had said, "Sorry, I'm new on the route, you know, musta missed that story." And Harold got to thinking about what Puck had said. Well, it made sense. Now all Harold had to do was make sense of it.

The '73 Chevy was lightly dusted with snow when Harold got home, but he brushed it off with his jacket sleeve, opened the trunk, and dug around looking for the brown box. He had not looked in it for years, and it was buried under piles of clothes, *Mad* magazines, old *TV Guides*, discarded kitchen gadgets given him by Snooky, and a plastic bag holding ten choir robes handed him by some lady he did not know who had appeared briefly one Sunday at the Catholic Summer Chapel and who left, as quickly as she appeared, never to return. The robes were purple and green, and Harold figured if he ever found his voice again, he would dig them out and start a town choir of his own. He pulled one out, shook it out, held it up, and was delighted to realize that it would solve the problem of his Joseph costume quite nicely. All I need now is a crown, he thought. Everyone would say, "Oh, Harold where did you get *that*?" And of course he would not be expected to answer them. There were advantages to being struck mute, sometimes.

After some minutes of digging in the trunk, Harold finally unearthed the box and tugged it out. He set it down on the snow-dusted ground and squatted beside it. He removed the top. Inside were, first, several neckties, very nice ones; a Bible written in some foreign language; a belt; a can of shoe polish; an empty candy box; a bundle of Christmas cards; a map of Europe, carefully folded; a postcard of a boat called "The Titanic"; some spoons held together with a rubber band; and a little red book with "The Continuing Diary Of . . . " printed on the first page. The "of" had never been filled in, but flipping it to the next page, Harold recognized Mr. Kringle's handwriting from the grocery notes of long ago. Harold turned over the contents of the box carefully. Not much promising here. No matching emerald rings, no code books, no secret letters, no invisible ink, no silver daggers. He sighed in disappointment, and decided to put it all back and give up.

But the light was fading fast and the air was uncomfortably chilly. Harold decided to build a fire, first. He got up, collected a few dry twigs from under the car where he kept his kindling and wood, arranged the twigs in a neat triangle in his fire ring, and lit a wooden match. The twigs blazed quickly and Harold fanned the fire with the little red book. Opening it, he tore out a page and fed it to the flame, which turned orange and then blue. It was so pretty that Harold tore out another page and tossed it on the fire. In the darkness, the flames flickered brightly.

Harold was about to toss on another page when he caught sight of the word "Harold." Sure enough, it said "Harold." His heart pounding, Harold lowered the book to his lap. He knew it was wrong to read someone else's diary. But was it wrong to read the diary of someone already dead?

Harold wished he could go ask Father. But by now Father would have had his bath and his Ovaltine and would be in bed. And Snooky was either taking his bath or cleaning up the kitchen or was wrapped in his blue robe in front of the fire, eating chocolate cherries and watching a show. Or reading his *Spain* book. Harold was worried and confused. Still, he had seen the word "Harold." Was it okay to read somebody's diary if it was about you? Maybe he could ask Honus, but even as he had that thought, the answer came to him. It would be all right to read only the parts with his name in them. That is what he would do.

He opened the book again, and with his finger keeping track, read down every page until he came to "Harold." Then he re-read that page.

> Olga has somehow stolen Harold's baseball card. At least she is teasing me about it. I am now sorry I told her about that particular visit from him, and that, to make him happy, I told him it was worth much money. How would I know? At any rate, she seems to have taken me seriously, and I must try to see if she is serious and if so, get the card back by shaming her for tormenting a simple person. Sometimes, she has not such a good character as I could wish. Or, she gets bored in this place, perhaps.

Harold's eyes bugged. So, now he knew. It wasn't Mr. Kringle who took Honus that time, but that lady who sometimes came late at night in a big car and stayed sometimes. Harold knew he should close the book right now. But, this wasn't really a clue yet, so he ought to try to read some more. He would just read a little more, he decided.

> I have bought a present for this little town. It will be a huge surprise for them all. When will it be delivered? I look forward to seeing their faces when it drives up. Olga says I am foolish. Perhaps I am. But a Mercedes! So much better than these things made in—where is it?—Detroit?

The fire was dimming. Harold tore that page from the book and tossed it on his bed of coals, added a few more twigs. It flared up, and Harold realized if he was going to keep the fire going, he would have to read quickly.

> I am afraid my little friend Glinda knows about Olga. Olga, like a sensible girl, just laughs at my peccadilloes. Ah well, a bit of heartbreak early, that is good for a young woman. Glinda's cousin, too, she follows me about with those hungry eyes. Am I flattered? If so, I am much too old for such silliness. Women

interest me, however. Can they sense these things? Certainly, I never tell them much.

Harold frowned. That was boring, and certainly didn't seem like a clue. What was Mr. Kringle talking about?

Olga did not come home tonight, but where could she have gone? She has not called, did not leave a note. Her car is here, all her things, as far as I can tell. But she is not here. Another lover? Another thing she threatens me with, possibly out of boredom also. Ah, as the poet says 'comfort me with apples, for I am sick of love.' I suspect I am. Age. However, I am worried. I suppose she was here at some point during the evening—a half empty glass of wine, a plate of cookies. Women.

Harold tore out that page and placed it on the glowing coals. It too blazed up orange and blue. He bent over in the flare, read the next page:

Two days now, and still no word from my pet. All her things are here. This is not like her to be hysterical. Would she just leave like this, no note, no talk? I hesitate to write, no recriminations, no scene? But her car is here, her clothes, her clutter. I am concerned, and—however, she is an adult woman and will do as she thinks best. No doubt she will—ach, this house is too noisy at night. Perhaps it is Olga returning and

And with that the diary ended. Harold thumbed through the blank pages. He sighed. No clues here. Well, Puck was wrong about this. Harold decided being a detective was not much fun. He tossed the little red book on the coals and watched it burn slowly. He rubbed his hands over the heat and sat staring into the darkness. Falling snow hissed as it hit the fire. An owl hooted in the woods and Harold felt comforted by the familiar sound. He was not Harold Mosby, Man Detective. I am just plain Harold. But then, I am more than that, he thought. I am Joseph in the Christmas play. And it is almost Christmas. Harold hooted back at the owl.

He stomped on his fire and scattered the coals and climbed

into his car. Just as he was drifting into sleep, warm in his bag, he had a question. How did Honus end up back in his red blanket piece if Gunther's lady friend had taken him? Floating in his sleepy twilight, Harold decided it didn't matter, not after all this time. Life was full of strangeness. You just couldn't worry about it all the time.

114

Part III
Chapter XI

Snooky Cooks Thanksgiving Dinner
And Adele and Glinda Have a Talk

When Snooky composed his Thanksgiving dinner menus, he rejected Julia's videos in favor of guidance from his ancestors. He doubted that French people had Thanksgiving at all, which was probably the reason Julia didn't seem to understand it. His great-aunt Charlotte's *Savannah Cookery* (thanks to the Junior League of her year) was propped in a plastic cookbook holder on his counter and open to a recipe for onions in sherry sauce. The page was brittle, spotted, yellow around the edges: small boiling onions, 2 tbs. (not enough, he thought) dry sherry, 1 teas. powd. mustard, 1 cup heavy cream, 1 stick butter, 1 pinch . . . 1 pinch . . . what? A mealybug, a silver fish, had eaten the grease spot over a pinch of what. Snooky guessed nutmeg, or mace, and deciding that mace was more festive, reached up into his cupboard for the little can.

Though really, he thought, could it make much difference to Harold? Two weeks ago, despite everything going on, he sat down and made up the guest list: Padre, Me, Adele, Her Cousin (if still in town), four. Maybe just three. A small fat turkey would do.

But as soon as he figured "four," and began making his shopping list—2 jars boiling onions, 4 yams, 1 bag marshmallows, 1 (2?) bags stuffing—he felt guilty. Who would feed Harold? Who would invite Buzz? Well nobody, naturally. Naturally, it would be his responsibility as per usual. He tore the top sheet off his memo pad, crumpled it up, and began again: Padre, Me, Adele, Her Cousin, Harold, Buzz, six. Medium—15 lbs.?—Butterball, 4 jars onions, 8 yams, 3 large bags h. stuffing, 2 cans jellied cran., 1 pk.

celery hearts, 2 cans pie squash, pecan halves, 3 cans creamed corn, mints, mayo (real), vanilla, 2 bottles decent sherry, 2 cans stuffed olives. (Mashed potatoes, too? If so, half potatoes, half parsnips, his grandmother's recipe.) Butter (2 lbs.), get parsnips, 2 cans mushrooms (whole or caps *only*), marshmallows.

Dinner—a word Snooky reserved for these holiday occasions—was for four o'clock. As soon as he had made out the shopping list, he called Adele to invite her and "bring your cousin, too, if she's free." He'd found Buzz at the Store. He'd gone to Harold's car to leave a note, but saw Harold sleeping inside, so he knocked on the window and Harold sat up in his sleeping bag and opened the flange and listened to the invitation, nodded, thought he might. Well, thought he probably could. He smiled and waved a "yes." His smile said he was some looking forward to it. Climbing back up the slippery bank from Harold's car, Snooky slid and hit his knee on a little stump. When he got home, he called Adele and told her he was keeping his knee elevated. That is, if he got a chance to sit down.

Adele did not seem herself lately, hadn't for weeks, not since this whole thing started. She seemed preoccupied, silent, almost unneighborly. He bustled around his kitchen this cold holiday morning, basting and peeling and consulting his lists, but worried about Adele the whole time. Maybe a good dinner would cheer her up.

They'd had Thanksgiving dinner together for so many years now, so he knew she especially liked creamed corn and had added an extra can. She also liked foil-wrapped after-dinner mints, so those were already arranged in a fan shape on a small silver plate. He had carved radishes into roses and celery sticks into little frills. The squash pies would be decorated with flutings of whipped cream, and the chess pie with a circle of pecan halves. What else could he do? Had he forgotten anything? He rechecked his menu. No, everything under control. Adele was going to enjoy this, and that would cheer her up.

But, he had his doubts, and doubts were something Snooky did not like very much, though he would now and then entertain them on behalf of his friends. What Adele really needed was for this thing to get over with. Everything just needs to get back to normal, he thought. Then she'll be all right again. Gerald can take us into town to do some Christmas shopping. We can help with the Library Christmas Tea and Carol Party. She can help me unwrap the tree ornaments. We'll go down to the Hall and offer to help with the costumes. But first, that cousin has to go back where she came from. That was his darkest thought, and he didn't like it a bit. That cousin was up to no good, but exactly what no good was she up to? Why hadn't she already left? Had that Sergeant Celted told her to stay in town until this silly murder was solved?

Vanity was only one of Snooky's poses, like his exasperation, like his exhaustion. So, although he knew Glinda thought he was a twit, a fussbudget, and a jester, none of that bothered him at all. He didn't like *her*. He didn't like her lipstick, her zippered boots, her bad grammar, and her small blue eyes hard as marbles. He didn't approve of red cars. He thought worldly people like Glinda had motives which didn't bear looking into, and he didn't like that either.

A few days ago he'd gone next door on the pretext of needing a recipe (as if he'd ever need a recipe from Adele!) but really wanting to see Adele and know she was all right, and he had thought for an awful minute that Glinda was making eyes at him. She had answered the back door in her bathrobe, if you want to call it that. It was unbuttoned, too low for comfort. She laughed when she saw him, looked him up and down, laughed again, and invited him in. Adele was over at "that shop." Why didn't he join her, Glinda, in the "toasty old kitchen?" He declined, went back home, feeling smeared somehow, or like a snail pulling back into safety. She isn't the least bit like Adele, he thought. There's just something about her I don't like at all.

Luckily for all involved, Snooky did not have occasion to hear the words Glinda actually did use to describe him, and certainly they were not "twit" and "jester." Probably he knew they wouldn't be. For one thing, he could have predicted that neither word was in Glinda's vocabulary. Perhaps he preferred not to use the words he knew she might use, not even to himself. Perhaps he preferred to think otherwise. Everyone has a tiger self. Had Snooky heard Glinda's actual words about him—which she used to Adele—or had he known what even shorter, uglier, cliché little words went through Glinda's mind, or, much more than that, if Snooky had known for sure what plans Glinda thought she had for Adele, he could easily and gracefully kill her in a clean, fierce way that would surprise everyone in town, including himself. Probably even surprise a few folks in San Francisco.

Weapon of choice? Snooky has many at hand: meat forks, cork-screws, cast-iron stewpots, a battery of the sharpest knives. At this moment he is smashing garlic buds (for the slaw), still in their papery peel, with the flat side of a heavy cleaver. He moves like a samurai. The washed steel blade of his blender, deadly as some-thing twirled in jungle warfare, stands drying at his elbow. If you think about it, a fifteen-pound turkey, stuffed, could probably do some damage if used with enough force. At least it could put a human target off balance.

But as it is, Snooky is simply cooking and fussing and watch-ing the timer. Worried about dinner, and about his friend Adele. My best friend. Well, minus the Old Holy. And Harold, of course; Buzz, I guess; Julia, in a way. Which reminds him to make a note to write cousin Jason, maybe send him a box of Maine-made some-thing for Christmas. Maybe a balsam wreath, too. Maybe Adele has some of those lovely maple-sugar suckers in the shape of lob-sters over at the shop again this year. It must be so lonely, living like Jason, in San Francisco. Meantime, six salad forks, six bun plates. Drain onions, boil in plain water until fork tender. In 1 stick of unsalted butter, melt ½ cup grated cheddar or other hard cheese, add teas. of mustard, dash of Tabasco, pint of cream, splash of sherry, pinch of . . . mace. Mix with drained onions and pour all into buttered oven dish, oval. Bake at 350° for 40 minutes or until golden. Let Pussums out. Baste the turkey.

Suddenly, Adele got up from the old brown wing-back, shuffled over to the TV set, and switched it off, right in the middle of a

Pepsi commercial featuring surfers, one of whom looked like Marc. Glinda, who had been following it with more attention than she'd given to all of Snooky's dinner, jerked upright.

"What the hell?" she asked.

"What the hell, indeed," said Adele. "We need to have a talk."

"Well, not now, Addie, I'm just too goddamn stuffed to think."

"That's too bad, because we have to talk anyway. And I'd rather you didn't call me that."

"Addie? Come on, I always called you that."

"Never. And don't start something now, Glinda. Just don't."

"Well, if that's the way you're going to be, I'm going to bed. I've had about enough of you and your funny chums for one day. Jesus, Adele, I know this is a hick town but there's gotta be some-body to hang out with besides senile old creeps and fairies and deaf-and-dumb hoboes and . . . "

"Shut up, Glinda, shut up and sit down and shut up." Adele almost whispered this, and it scared Glinda enough to follow di-rections. She sat back down, and the cousins sat there, in silence, looking at the blank screen. The clock ticked, with the limp it has always had, the tick too fast, the tock too slow. The faucet dripped in the kitchen. Sleet clicked against the windows. Both women were deeply afraid, so Glinda's mind began to wander. A black-and-white TV in this day and age? My God, is this the twentieth cen-tury, or what? This has got to be the cheapest, shittiest, cheesiest place in the world, must be. What would Marc think of this hole, this . . . oh, get it over with.

"Well," said Glinda, "what?"

"You know 'what,'" said Adele, still in that near whisper, "and now we're going to talk about it. How long do you think the police are going to buy all this malarkey before they catch on? We haven't even been telling the same story. I don't know all you've been telling them, and I'm so mixed up by now I don't know what I've been telling them, either, but I think this is it, Glinda. And I think we better get this worked out, and good, and face some facts here. And I think we'd better start with what you've said to that Detec-tive, word-for-word."

Glinda thought. She didn't know for sure, what she had said. Panic came up in her throat like a taste of vomit. Well, after a hideous dinner like that, why wouldn't it? Then she realized her mind was changing the subject.

"Tell when?" she said, pouting, as of yore.

"Any time, Glinda, any time you have talked to them. What you told them at any time, exactly what you said."

"I said I didn't know."

"From the beginning."

"I said I didn't know. That I was leaving town. That my purse got stolen. At the dance. Remember that dance?"

"There was no dance, remember? We made that up. You made that up. There was no dance," said Adele.

"Look, okay, there was no dance. Did you ask me if there was? You said tell you what I said for Chrissakes, so this is it, I'm telling you. I said I was leaving town. I went to the dance. My purse was stolen. The ring was in the purse. That's all I know. I never saw this person before."

"What person? Start again. What date was that? That's the kind of thing they notice, you realize. Dates. Times. Alibis are checked by dates and things like that. I'm telling you, Glinda, today's a holiday but tomorrow isn't, and they are going to be back on the job and we have got to present a united front so our stories had better match up. If you can't get that through your head, Glinda, you are stupider than I ever realized."

Glinda began to cry a little, and sniffed. "Jesus, Adele, I come back for a visit. I get to thinking about the good old days, and Gram and Gramps, and you. And the first thing that happens is my own goddamn funeral and then all this mess, and I just wish you'd try to see my side of things for once. What do you want from me? How much of this do you think I can stand?"

"What I want is simple. I want our stories to match up. Surely you can see that our stories have to match up. So forget all that other for a minute, and anyhow, I don't believe it. Concentrate. Tell me what you've told them."

"I told them at the dance somebody stole my purse. I didn't

know who. You bought me a new ticket and I got the bus the next day and never knew what happened after that except later you wrote me, I think I said, and told me Gunther had passed away. I told them I've been gone ever since and just came back to see you. For old times' sake. That I had no idea."

"No idea what?"

"No idea about the body! Or how it could've got hold of my purse and ring. Or died. That I didn't know anything."

"Do you remember telling them any days, dates? Wednesday, Tuesday?"

"No. Why would I tell them any date? How am I supposed to remember a goddamn date?"

"Because of the bus ticket. They found the bus ticket, remember? If it's for a Tuesday, but you said Wednesday—that's what I'm trying to get through your head."

"Adele, not everybody is pick-pick-pick like you. The police think big, like who is the body and all that. So why don't you relax and try to think big, Adele, which is something *you've* never been able to do."

It was getting cold in the room. Adele got up again, opened the stove lid, raked the coals, added two small logs. Dusting her hands on her hips, she went out to the kitchen, returned with a bottle of rum and two jelly glasses, and poured a little rum into each. She handed one to Glinda, who took it. Adele sat down again, drank her rum in one swallow, and put the glass on a magazine on the high table between the two wing-back chairs. She cleared her throat.

"What day was it?"

"What day was what?"

"*The* day."

"The day we did it?"

"'*We*' didn't do it, Glinda, if you remember correctly. I did it."

"*You* did it? *I* did it!"

"What are you talking about, Glinda? I did it."

"Adele, you really make me sick. What do you want—credit for everything?"

"If I say I did it, I mean I did it."

"Yah, and who else? your terrific friends? your deaf-'n-dumb buddy there? your preacher? your brilliant fat creepo pansy . . . " and Adele reached out and slapped Glinda, hard, twice.

"Shut up, I told you, and I mean it," Adele said. "This is neither here nor there. And I'm not getting into it now. Olga deserved it. She took him away from me. If not for her, he'd have loved me, me, I tell you."

"If not for her! I like that! I was the one he loved, and she was in my way. Fiddle-dee-dee and crapola. It was *me*. And I killed her."

"If you killed her so you could have him, Glinda, then tell me why you had your bus ticket all bought and were running out of town, tell me that. You're just horning in on somebody else's life, as usual, and I wish you'd mind your own business."

"Adele your brain is like a fucking sieve. I told you—I had a plan. I kill her. She dies. Meantime, I'm gone. Of *course* I was leaving. Did you think I'd stick around and wait to be arrested? I'd just murdered somebody, right? But if I'm out of town when it happens, how could I be the murderer? See? The bus ticket was my alibi. Then, I hear she's dead, I come back—say for the funeral or something—and there I am and the coast is clear. And Gunther and I get married, move to Europe or someplace, and that's that. And Adele, if we're going to get down to the nitty-gritty here, then how come you didn't try to kill me, and not her? I mean, I was the one so-called 'standing' between you and your big love."

"I didn't know that then, Glinda. I didn't know."

"Didn't know, didn't know, and so where did you think I'd gotten this ring? Crackerjack?"

"You said, you bought it for yourself."

"Uh-huh. A gold and emerald ring, an emerald this big. Look at it, Adele. I bought an emerald this big on my fabulous salary as a shampoo girl? Face life, would you?"

"Look, Glinda, let's not get into all that. So, he was a two-timer . . . "

"Three-timer, sweetie, three-timer!" And Glinda went off in

peals of hiccupping wet laughter. "Three-timer, three-fucking-timer, if you really count yourself. But I'll hand it to you for one thing. She did have it coming. And I don't know how he died exactly, the bastard, but he had it coming, too. But I say and I'll say it again, it was your shitty old dandelion wine which I doctored up with something in the shed, that's what did it, and don't you forget it."

"And how do explain that half the cookies were gone?"

"Adele, you make me sick. How could rat, or whatever, poison still be good after getting cooked in a hot oven. You've got to be kidding. Besides, who would eat anything you'd cooked? She probly gave them to that ugly dog of hers and he was still plenty alive that night, if you recall. God, Adele, remember how he tried to follow us to the dump? God, was that a scene—remember? I was trying to drag her down the back steps, and that fucking dog kept whining and whining. You tried to shut him up and started kicking him back into the house. And then those lights went on across the street, and God, what a night that was to remember. When we bumped into each other in the dark, trying to look in the kitchen window to see if she was dead yet, God, I nearly shit my pants, I swear."

"You're an idiot, Glinda. And I wish you'd watch your mouth." Adele picked up the rum bottle. "Here, we need it. But you know, that's what stays with me about that night. Kicking that poor dog. I've thought about that a lot. That's what I feel bad about. Kicking that dog that night. Odd. You'd think killing a, well, you'd think kicking a dog was not something that'd stay with you so long."

"You promised, Adele, that nobody would ever find out. You promised that nobody knew about you and Gunther, not that you had anything like what him and I had going, you promised. You swore that nobody knew her at all. You swore we buried her deep enough. You swore that nobody would ever use that part of the dump again. You promised, Adele, you promised, and now look at all this." And Glinda was really sobbing.

"And nobody did, did they? They don't know now, Glinda, so pull yourself together. There is nothing to tie us in with it if we get our stories to match up. She's dead. He's dead. For that matter, the dog's dead. There is not one particle of evidence if we keep our heads. So my point is not to dig all this up again, but just be sensible now, and get this over with. Nobody knows anything but you and me, and if we are smart, the whole thing is dead and gone. Can't you see that? So we don't need to go into all this, and you don't need to carry on like that. We just need to get our heads together."

"On what?"

"On the details. Do I really have to go through the whole thing over again? The details, Glinda. The dates. The facts. Well, the lies, I guess. The facts of the lies."

The two women, in their robes and slippers, sit shivering in the late-night room, with the small fire hissing, the sleet scratching the windows. They think their own thoughts. But their thoughts, at this moment, begin the same: "If not for her, I'd have . . . " and the big, handsome, rich, mysterious German man fills the cold room with his ghostly presence more powerfully than the Pepsi surfer resembled Marc. For both women, Gunther had been the real ticket out. But more than that, a true passion. Enough passion to have driven one sensible nature, one silly one, to making plans with household poisons as improbable as Snooky murdering a rival with a corkscrew. Nevertheless, they had carried it out. And if not for the accident of timing, they would never have discovered each other. All it took was a bump in the dark, under a kitchen window. What, you? And, you?

But it's not that terrible moment that both women remember now in this sleety, rum-smelling silence. They are each back in the months before that chill spring night, back in their by then separate bedrooms, watching, in the dark, the shadow of a third woman in silhouette, night after night, through the drawn shades of next door. Laughter, the silhouette, music, early darkness. They sit remembering the big black car. They hear Gunther saying, "Who, my darling? Ah, Olga! Olga, of course! My cousin, my darling. My cousin and my business associate. You must meet her one of these days, you must come for tea. You American girls. So suspicious of an old man." Adele gets up to poke the fire.

"Remember when he gave me the ring, Adele?"

"I guess so. I mean, I remember when you got it."

"The police gave it back to me."

"Yes, I see they did. That's nice."

"Did he ever give you anything, Adele?"

"In a way. Yes. In a way. But really, I'd rather not go into it."

"It's all over with, isn't it? I mean, it's just too long ago. I didn't really mean to kill her, Adele. I thought she'd just get sick or something, and blame Gunther, I guess, and leave. And I don't think you killed her, Adele. She just died, probably. But I don't think we should tell the police, do you? I mean our story makes sense. There's my purse, my bus ticket and everything. It makes sense, doesn't it? I see what you mean. We've got to tell them the same thing and we just about have, haven't we? A few details maybe, but only details. Adele, did you really not know about Gunther and I?"

"You know I didn't."

"And I didn't know you had a thing on him, Adele, you know I didn't know that. I thought that was just a high-school crush and was all over with. I thought it was only her. Her coming in between him and I." And Glinda began to cry again, but in a slightly crocodile way, with one eye on Adele. Adele did not notice.

"And I didn't know about you, either, Glinda. I'm glad I didn't, at the time. I really thought you were leaving, anyway. That's what you went around telling everyone for months and months."

"Well, yeah, I guess I did. I was going to leave, and then, like I said, come back and get him to marry me . . . "

"Let's not talk about it anymore, all right? It all seems so long ago, I wonder sometimes what it could have meant in the first place. Or why I could have been fond of him enough to kill her, when I look back."

"Well, you didn't."

"Didn't what?"

"Oh well, Addie, let's forget about it for tonight. Let's talk about it tomorrow if we need to. Let's make some new plans, tonight. Now, my idea is this. As soon as this is over with, let's you and I go back to Boston together. Just shut up this house for a few weeks, shut up your shop, give the cat to what's-his-face next door, and come back with me for Christmas. We should do this. Look at what a good time we've had in the past coupla weeks. In fact, the major reason I came back was to persuade you to come for a visit. I've got gobs of room. We can go shopping, just like in the old days. You seriously need a break, Adele. Look at you!"

"I don't know, Glinda, I just don't know. The shop's been closed for weeks. I really must get it open again, Christmas and all. I've got plans. I'd really have to think about it. Shopping? I don't know."

"Oh come on, Adele, what kind of plans could *you* have? You aren't getting any younger, you know! One Christmas, for a change, in the big time? There's some people I'd love you to meet, my girl-friend Tina, for instance. Great parties. Just a whirl. You'd love it. You owe it to yourself, for a change. I mean, I realize, Adele, we've got a lot more in common than I used to think we had. We could have a real family holiday for once."

In common? thought Adele, a family holiday? A family holiday would be the Library Christmas Tea, and unwrapping Snooky's decorations together over a teacup of eggnog. It would be helping with costumes at the Christmas Pageant, making sure Harold had his zipper up and his headdress on tight. Family would be the town's big Christmas tree, all lit up in the parking lot at the Store. It would be sitting in Gram's spot at church for Christmas Eve vespers. But, it was nice for Glinda to want her to come, and, it would be a change all right. But maybe a change would be good.

"Let me think about it for a day or two. It is an idea. Thanks, Glinda. I will think it over." And Adele got up, turned down the damper, said good night, and went up the stairs.

Glinda picked up the rum bottle, shook it, held it to the light, but it was empty. She, too, got up, looking a little drunk and hugely pleased. She walked crookedly into the kitchen intending to turn off the lights, but they were already off and she turned them on. Frowned. Turned them off again.

Next door, Snooky got up to check on the Padre, saw the kitchen lights flicker at Adele's, and hoped that everything over there was all right and nobody was up in the night with indigestion because of his good dinner. All over town everything was in darkness and sleet hissed down all night. Next morning, the roads would be impossible. But that would be okay because there was no school anyway, and everyone would have lots of leftovers for supper.

Glinda went into the back bedroom and eased into the damp, thin, mended sheets and heavy pile of scratchy brown blankets, vowing, as is often the case when too much rum hits very cold sheets, that tomorrow she'd be a better person. The sooner I cooperate, she told herself, the sooner this will *all* be over and I can get back to my Honey Buns. She snuggled down, trying to get warm, thinking of her Honey Buns in his own lonely bed, having spent a dutiful Thanksgiving Day with his mom. Just as he said he was going to do. Whereas Marc is, even at this quite late hour, at a club dancing off shrimp scampi with Traci. He has not thought of Glinda for weeks, why should he?

But Glinda's bedtime pleasure, despite the cold sheets, is based on Marc's loneliness for her. She has sent him a lot of funny postcards over the past few weeks, but just to say "hi." One of a moose looking into an outhouse, one of a huge potato on a tiny flatcar, one of clams trying to make love with a funny saying on it. But she hasn't told him what's been going on. She'll save that for later. She didn't think he'd be able to understand what was funny about her funeral.

His longing for her, as she imagines it, stokes her resolve, her conviction that, having dragged one dead body down a granite stoop, she can certainly do it again. The trunk of the new red car is deceptively roomy. She will tell everyone in town that she and Adele plan to leave before it gets light so as to miss morning rush hour getting into Boston. If anyone in town even misses Adele after a few months of absence, a couple of cards with a scrawled "A" will reassure them she's still living it up in civilization. Soon, they'll forget her. If they think of her at all. Which Glinda doubts.

Someday in the rosy future, Glinda—and Marc, by that time— will come back to Bosky Dells for a day to put the house in Puck's hands. She'll give Puck a key. Tell him to arrange for an auction of the things. Tell him and everyone else (that cutey poops next door, for example) that dismantling the old family place was too sad for Adele to face, so she had stayed in Boston but sent them her best. No one would think otherwise. Pretty soon—Glinda hadn't got this part figured out yet, but intended to work on it—the money would be hers. The property would be hers. The money from the sale of the house would be hers. Marc would be hers. She'd been practicing Adele's signature for months. The years would roll by; everyone would forget.

Though Glinda didn't think she'd risk a second dump burial, tomorrow she'd figure out where to stash her cousin's body. That and a weapon. But hell, weapons were all over the place. Meantime, the bed began to warm up; Glinda burrowed down as far as she could get, and slept at last.

Chapter XII

In Which Adele Decides to Go on a Trip

Upstairs, in her also cold bed, Adele lay thinking about Glinda's invitation. For a reason she couldn't understand, though she tried to do so, she wanted to believe her cousin this once. Glinda was as silly as ever, but did seem somehow nicer. Adele wanted to believe they could have a good time in Boston, if only for a few weeks. She wanted to believe that something could change, that life did not have to be stuck in routine all the time. She had never seen the lights of a city at holiday time. The stores. The windows. The decorated streets. She tried to imagine what it was like. Shimmering. Magical. Luminous. All those Irving Berlin-type words.

Why shouldn't she take some time off? The reality was that she didn't really need the little bit of income she'd get from the shop between now and the holidays. She really didn't need money at all, if truth were told. She had her nest egg, that nice sum Gram had left her. Just her. Not a cent to Glinda. She wondered if Glinda knew about that, and felt a momentary flush of guilt.

Though why she felt guilty, she didn't understand, either. It hadn't been her doing that the grandparents had left her the money, the house. And the woodlot. And the lake property with a couple miles of frontage. Not a cent or an acre to Glinda. Nor had Glinda ever read or heard about or asked about any will, nor responded with a note or call or anything when Adele had written to tell her Gram had died.

And of course nothing so dramatic as "a reading of the will to the assembled" had taken place, as Adele, from reading mysteries, had thought it probably would. No, the day after Gram's funeral, Adele had simply gone to the lawyer's office and he had simply handed her a file folder tied with a string and had simply said, "I think you ought to know what this says and then we'll talk about where you stand." Before listing all they were leaving to Adele, and the trust they were leaving to the Library and for the upkeep of the cemetery lot, Gram and Gramps had stated that "nothing further" was to go to Glinda, on the grounds that "We have done our best by her."

Adele supposed they had, in their way. She turned over in bed, looked at the clock's glowing numbers: 2:37. She suddenly remembered the incident of the braces.

Glinda, at age sixteen or thereabouts, on the floor, having a tantrum. Gram, standing and wringing her hands around a dish towel. Adele watching from the doorway. Gramps sitting in his chair, refusing to take notice, pretending to read his newspaper. "I'll kill myself, I swear I will, you'll see, you'll be sorry then, I will, I will," sobbed Glinda.

The scene had begun after supper with Glinda announcing she had to get braces. Then Gramps looking up from his paper and asking "Braces? What's those?" And Glinda screaming and running from the room and running back with a movie magazine and holding it close to Gramps' face and yanking it open to a set of perfect white teeth and then pointing to the wide gaps between her own. "See? See? See these horrible teeth?" she shrieked, "Look at this, would you? This can get *fixed*, you know. Do you want my life to be ruined? I'll kill myself!"

The old man had studied Doris Day's smile on the slick page, squinted up at Glinda's open mouth, looked back at the page, and then glanced over to his wife and shrugged, as if to say: you'd be the one to handle this. Gram had started to handle it by saying that Glinda was still growing and her teeth would probably fill in nicely one of these days, whereupon Glinda had thrown herself face-first onto the brown carpet and beat her fists and feet, screaming that she'd *kill* herself if they forced her to live looking this hideous. Did they want to *kill* her?

Of course Gram and Gramps had given in, together had looked for "orthodontist" in the Yellow Pages, had written the checks. Thinking about that scene now, Adele recalled watching the little puffs of dust that rose from the carpet. She remembered feeling nothing but cold scorn. She licked her own teeth, across the fronts. She had nice teeth then, still did. How often, all her life, Glinda had used the word "kill" as though it were the simplest solution in the world. "I could just kill her." "It just killed me." "I would kill for a date with him." "I'll kill myself and then you'll be sorry." "What a killer that was." "Do you want me to kill you?" And so forth.

After the clothes, the food, the braces, the wear and tear of raising her—no, not one penny left to Glinda. Interesting, because when the old folks wrote the will, Glinda was still living in their house, causing trouble, picking on Adele, having tantrums, flunking classes, staying out all night, making endless demands, getting her way, doing her baby act afterwards. "Tank-oo Gwammy, kiss for widdo Gwinda?" And Adele would see the uneasy combination of disgust and worry cross her grandmother's small old face as she took the willful girl into her arms and added a little pat.

All that money, and she, Adele, had it. But, she could do a few nice things for her cousin now, if this Christmas visit worked out. Maybe buy a few things for Glinda's apartment. Adele assumed it was an apartment. A new fridge, maybe, if she needed one. Or one of those CD music players. Glinda would probably like that a lot. Or tickets for a boat cruise, or was that called a cruise boat? Glinda had told her how she'd given up taking a cruise just to visit Bosky Dells because she was concerned about Adele. That was very nice of Glinda. Adele could afford a cruise for the two of them. Yes, someplace warm, just after Christmas.

Probably the big boats left right from Boston Harbor. She could surprise Glinda with the tickets under the tree. She could put them in an envelope, but then put the envelope in a great big box, all wrapped up. Glinda would be fooled by that. Maybe, they would meet two nice men on board, have a little shipboard romance. Adele smiled at the idea. Saw herself for a minute, dancing under a tropical moon. Sitting in a deck chair, reading an Agatha Christie and drinking iced tea with a sprig of mint. There'd be games on board, and she could put her feet in the pool. Go ashore some quaint and colorful native island and buy Snooky a nice present, a basket or something. Maybe get Gerald and his wife a present, too. What would they like?

I deserve a holiday, she thought. Basically, I've been a good person all my life. I've taken care of this house. I haven't wasted the money. I took care of Gram. I took care of Glinda. I sacrificed my own career. I might have been something. But I was a good person, instead. Just one—mistake—that shouldn't be held against a person forever. Besides, Glinda's right for once. Olga, what-her other-name-was, shouldn't have done what she did. So pretty, so blond, such pretty clothes, so—tall. She'd weighed a ton when they had dragged her down the back steps in the dark, dragged her up onto Gramps' pickup. It was still running then, and Glinda could drive. More than a ton when they'd dragged her out, dug the hole at the dump, a huge hole. Or so it had seemed that night, towards the cold spring dawn.

A thin line of gray along the eastern horizon had turned coral. A rooster crowed. Rats were everywhere. The dump smoked and stank, stank to high heaven, sickening. Was heaven "high?" And was this Olga woman, waiting under a plastic tarp for her hole to be dug, already up there? For once, Glinda had pitched in with the other shovel. For once, not whined about having cramps or having just done her nails. Both—well, girls, they were then—dug furiously in the grit, filth, cinders, mud, garbage. Eyeing each other: could she kill? did I kill? is this person dead? could I have done this? will we get this done? will someone come along? will we get away with this?

And then wasted precious minutes while it got lighter and lighter, arguing about whether or not to leave the ring, too. "Okay, Adele, I understand—my purse, my one and only ticket, but my ring, too? I love this ring! Why has it got to be my ring? Look at this Christly hole! Who is ever going to find her? And we've gotta bury my ring, too? It's because you hate me, that's why, isn't it? You hate me because Gunther loves me and doesn't give you the time of day, isn't that it?" But Adele had prevailed, had bullied, had insisted, had threatened: the ring, too. "Take it off, Glinda, and put it on that finger. I don't care if you don't want to touch a dead body. Just do it. Do it right now."

And Glinda, blubbering with rage, fear, and confusion, had kissed the ring good-bye, actually kissed it, and put it on the finger of Olga's body. Where it wouldn't go down. Glinda sobbed wildly. Adele hit her, and turned to the body, picked up the fat, white, heavy, stiff hand and jammed the ring and jammed it, and finally spit on the finger, rubbed the spit around, and holding the hand between her knees, forced the emerald down to the last joint. And said, "There," just as though she'd finished planting the peas or bringing in the last armload of wood. Glinda thought the spit was revolting, thought Adele was beyond disgusting. Adele thought Glinda was incompetent and a baby. Neither girl was thinking: somehow, between us, we have killed and are now burying a human being. Whoever she was, whatever she has done or failed to do, she probably didn't have this coming.

Even at that moment, I was planning a good deed, thought Adele. Thinking of taking care of my own. Olga was a thief. Perhaps not enough to get killed about, but a thief just the same. Imagine taking Harold's baseball card. Why would a person want to do that? What a thing to do! Even in that dawn, digging that hole, burying the body, I kept patting my pocket, making sure the card was still there. And later, shaking in my boots, didn't I sneak to Harold's and put the card where I knew he had kept it? I knew it was Harold's only treasure. I knew Olga had stolen it when we found it in her pocket. Harold would never have given it away. How can you steal from somebody like Harold? What would she want with an old baseball card, anyhow? I could have just thrown it away. No, I gave it back. I've been a good person. Even at my worst, I was still good.

Boston wouldn't be forever, just a few weeks, just for Christmas. She could explain it to Snooky. He would understand. Maybe it would even poke him into taking that long-overdue trip to San

Francisco he was always talking about, to visit that Jason. She would offer to help him trim the tree before she left. That would please him. She was sure he'd be willing to look after Fido for a little while. And after the holidays, no, after the cruise—yes, she would do that—then she would come home. Home to Bosky Dells and her house and her shop and her friends and her habits. But, for the rest of her life, she would know that she had done something different for a change. That would be nice to think about.

Then she could settle down again, reopen the shop, maybe build another room and stock it with—well, some nice books, some nice colorful books, like people put on their coffee tables. She had always wanted to sell books. She would have the shop painted, and the house painted, and yes—she would have new bathroom fixtures put in. Just in case the stay with Glinda worked out and Glinda ever wanted to visit her again. Why, they could switch off visits every other Christmas. People would say, "Oh, Adele? I think she's down to Boston for the holidays. Let's see, yep, Glinda was here last year. That means Adele's down to Boston 'til after the First."

The clock on the dresser read 4:12. Fido buried himself deeper in the blankets. The room was cold, her breath showed, but Adele was sweating with excitement. Calm down, she thought. Get some sleep. If you're going with Glinda, you've got a lot to do beforehand. Drain the pipes. Tell Mr. Cobbett to hold the mail. Arrange with Snooky about Fido. Call somebody on the Library committee and tell them I won't be here to help with the tea. Tell the costume committee to find someone else for the dress rehearsal and night of. Pack. You need to get some sleep.

Time marched on. Glinda's springs squeaked. Sleet clicked. The town's sand truck rumbled past, its yellow lights flashing. Better get used to bright lights, Adele thought. She closed her eyes and slept at last.

Chapter XIII

In Which Gerald and Sergeant Celted Go Deer Hunting
And the Case Is Officially Closed

Not everyone in town on this Thanksgiving Day had cooked and eaten and reminisced and gone to bed late. On this very same day, when all the rest of the U.S. of A. sat down to roasted turkey and squash pies drowning in Cool Whip, on this very same day when all his fellow countrymen were enjoying the fruits of their many labors, Gerald was stomping behind Sergeant Celted through the ice-cold November woods in search of a deer to shoot.

Not that Gerald wanted the meat for himself. He had already bagged three—one with his own tag, one with his wife's tag, and still another with his grandmother's. No, he certainly wasn't doing this to feed his family. He was doing it for some horse's-ass bigwig police chief in Boston that he'd never even met, and was not likely to, either. And on top of that, didn't want to meet, even if he ever got the chance.

Yesterday, he'd been sitting in his EMT/Deputy Office at the Fire House, thinking of closing up a little early on account've the holiday, when the stupid phone rang.

Long distance. The upshot being would he mind taking Thanksgiving Day off—(he thought he had it "off" as it was!)—to take Sergeant Celted hunting? Might be his last day up in those parts. (Which was news to Gerald.) (Did that mean Celted was calling it quits at last?) Sure would be doing the Chief a favor. (And who the eff are you?) Celt's a friend of his. Wouldn't hurt a bit, who'd you say you are? to have someone like the Chief on your side, in case, you know what I mean. (What the hell would he need a Boston cop on his side for? Did this twerp on the phone think he, Gerald, was going to commit a crime? or was dying to move to Boston? or even visit? Yvonne would never leave her two hundred and twenty-nine relatives to go anywhere for longer than eight hours. She even got nervous the coupla times they went to the Maine Mall for Christmas shopping for the kids, couldn't wait to get back home.) Well, if you'd have the time free, I'm sure the Chief would really dig a few venison steaks for the holidays. Thanks a lot. Tell Celt we all miss him. By the way, what kind of place is that, anyhow? Way up there, I bet. Well, thanks again. Click.

Terrific. So, there it was. He was going to take this hotshot pantywaist cop out to bag a deer, on Thanksgiving Day, with every one of Yvonne's two thousand relatives coming to his house for dinner and putting their porky little fingers into his pie. He told Yvonne on Wednesday night, just as they were getting into bed. "Jeez, Gerald, who are you married to? this town or me? On Thanksgiving. What'll I tell Mom? What'll I tell everybody? Seems to me, I empty bedpans and clean up drool at the job five, six days a week sometimes, that when I do get time off that you could spend it with your family. Maybe I should tell the kids the mailman is their daddy. At least they get to see him every day. Jeez, Gerald, I'm serious, Jeez. Can't you just say no?"

Well, she was right, he had to admit. All for a measly 20-thou a year. He'd make it up to her. Take her dancing at the Club Hulla-baloo this very Saturday night. Get her to get a baby sitter. He'd get somebody to cover for him; he'd wear his new jacket. She'd mentioned it last weekend, that "Lenny & The Leftovers" were playing this coming Saturday. Yeah, that would be the thing to do. He'd tell her tonight, after everybody left.

Gerald cast a cold eye at the clean-shaven neck of the man walking up the path in front of him. As if he would tell this jerk where the best hunting spots were. As if. Then every flatlander south of Biddeford would swarm all over town next year. Not likely he'd help this guy get one. Our deer, he thought. Then figured that was kind of a dumb thought, considering what the deer herd had done to every vegetable plot and fruit tree in town this year. "How's

your garden doin'?" "Do you mean did the deer enjoy my cabbages, my sprouts, my lettuce, my beans, my goddamn name it? I
surely do hope so." Gerald and Yvonne had kept a good eye on
their russet pear tree. Three, four bushels maybe, and the first year
it had borne. The Saturday morning they'd decided it was time to
pick the pears, they and the kids went out with the wheelbarrow,
the stepladder, some baskets, and thought they had the wrong tree.
Not a pear on any branch, not a pear on the ground, not a pear to
be seen. Gotta be the wrong tree. This tree had hundreds of perfect
pears on it. Yesterday? Yvonne, when did we look at this tree last,
yesterday? A rain, a wind in the night, the ripe and ready pears fell,
the herd came out of the woods and left nothing behind but
slightly flattened grass full of small droppings. Gerald's cousin
Natalie from out of state had said one time, "How can *anyone* shoot
even *one* little deer?" And Gerald had replied, "Beats me why
they'd just stop at one."

"Hope you got slugs for that gun," Gerald said flatly.

Celted patted the pocket of his hunting coat.

"Right here. Buckshot, too."

"Hope you loaded the gun."

"One barrel with buck, one with slugs. Just in case."

For a second, Gerald was impressed. Then he thought of his
dinner getting cold and stiff at home, cold, stiff, or else over-heated
and runny. Maybe they'd get lucky and a deer would jump right
out in front of them. Then if he dressed it out, he just might get
home in time for some pie before Yvonne's relatives ate it all.
Though he'd have to admit, though never out loud to anyone, that
cold stuffing, pulled from the bird with his fingers, late at night,
was the thing he liked best. That, and running his finger through
the carton of leftover Cool Whip. But he'd grumble to Yvonne about
all the pie being gone. For a split second, Gerald considered taking
his charge over to the salt licks, but at once thought better of it. He
didn't want to chance ending up dead and buried in the dump if
any of the other boys found out.

What was this guy's name, anyway? "Liam?" What the hell
kind of name was that? Was it "Lye-um? Lee-um?" And what did

anyone in town really know about him? Oh sure, he had the credentials. He was who he said he was. Had flashed his little badge about a thousand times now. But who was he? He kept to himself at the B & B. Never stopped at the Store for lunch. Never just wandered around town. Rode around in his little unmarked car. Didn't talk much, but smiled too much. Told somebody he was "Irish." Well, "Irish-American." What the eff did that mean? If you were an American you were an American, and if you weren't, you weren't. But you sure as hell couldn't be two things at once.

Gerald saw that the light was thinning. He could smell snow on its way, or maybe sleet. Yeah, a nice ice storm. Just what I need. His feet were sweating in his insulated pacs, but his butt was cold from sitting in the woods all morning waiting for a deer that had gone Christmas shopping, probably. And once his butt got cold, it wouldn't warm up until he could lower it down in a steaming tub of water.

"About twenty minutes," he said, aloud. "After that, won't be legal."

Not that he really gave a shit. The time of day didn't have a lot to do with it when your brother-in-law was warden, but this Celted guy seemed very stuck on following the rules, and it was getting dark, and he was frigging cold, and there was still a slim chance he'd get home in time for dinner. Yvonne would appreciate that.

"Well, we gave it the old college try," Celted said, turning around. "May as well start back."

Gerald's heart jumped for joy, joy, and a drumstick.

"Might just as well," he agreed, and tried to hide his relief. Down the path towards town they went, Gerald leading the way. He checked his watch. Quarter to four. Almost dark. His spirits rose with each step.

"Maybe you'd like to stop by for a piece of Yvonne's pie and some coffee," he offered.

"Thanks, I'd love to, but actually I've got something I want to get wrapped up. I've been planning to talk it over with you all afternoon. I've been studying this murder case you have here in town, you know. If murder it was. I think we must assume that it was. I've asked, as you know, many questions. And I've had some excellent help at the labs, and so on. Details. Now everything seems to fit together very neatly, actually. A few holes. I'd like to tell you our conclusions, if we could just, ah, sit down for a moment."

Oh, let's do that, thought Gerald. But let's give it the old college try, and find a really nice wet spot, okay? Let's locate a swamp and sit down in that. Sure, got all day. No problem.

"Sure, no problem. How about right here?" Gerald and Celted sat down with their backs against a damp red pine. Celted fished in the many pockets of his canvas jacket, pulled out a pipe, a bag that said "Celted" on it. Jesus, thought Gerald, special blend, yet. Celted filled the pipe, tapped it in, and closed the bag. Gerald waited. Celted fished again, brought out a wooden match, stuck it on the edge of a NO HUNTING sign, nearly twisted in half, lying on the ground. He puffed, looked into his pipe, pulled, puffed, looked, pulled.

"How 'bout a Marlboro?" Gerald offered his box.

"Never touch the stuff, but thanks," Celted said. Odd, thought Gerald, how his eyes seem to have no color at all.

"Yes, very neatly, I'd say. I won't bore you with the details, which anyway I think we have pretty well fitted together. It seems, well, I'll sum it up for you from the beginning. You had a German citizen living here in this town at one time. Right?"

Gerald nodded.

"Now, not too many people seemed to have known much about him. As a matter of fact, he wasn't German, though everyone seems to have thought so, but from Alsace-Lorraine. That's what I mean by details. At any rate, he kept rather to himself, am I right again?"

Gerald nodded again, wondered where this was going. A geography lesson right here in the frozen woods, maybe? *Twenty Questions*?

"We ran a check on him. Quite possible to do, you know. And, as it turns out, the case is quite classic. This man Kringle, came to town, as far as we can determine, for the purpose of conducting illegal activities. Think about it: a small, out of the way place—perfect—an unsophisticated population."

"Asshole," Gerald murmured in his head. "And the Nazi subs came ashore in Machias, too."

"If it were today," Celted continued, "we'd immediately suspect drugs. But thirty years ago? We thought, not likely. Possible, but not likely. We've pretty much been able to pin down that he was involved in prostitution."

Gerald laughed out loud. "A whorehouse? In the village? Who the hell in this town would go to a whorehouse? You guys've gotta hair. The only whore we ever had here was old Mabel Bryant and Jesus, she did it for free! Or, for a half-cord or so."

"No, you misunderstand me. Kringle certainly wasn't employing local gir . . . women. And his clientele weren't you local boys. Not at all. And in a sense, there was no 'house' if you see what I mean. Oh no, the, ah, women were from, you could say, around the world. Global. And his clients were, insofar as we can put it together, influential gentlemen from corporate America. Men who could afford the very best, but couldn't afford indiscretion, if you see what I'm saying. Happens all the time. I might add, not around here, no doubt. But Kringle's house here was simply, we believe, a discreet headquarters, or retreat, as it were, in a sense."

Celted paused, scratched another match on the twisted sign, puffed and pulled on his pipe.

"And?" said Gerald.

"And," puff, pull, puff, "and, one of his employees decided to rat on him. Or, maybe she got sick of her job and wanted out. Or, maybe she resented him. Who knows? For that matter, it really isn't our MO to second-guess these things. Or, maybe she got romantically involved with one of his clients. Or wanted to quit this line of work and marry—and had to be silenced—blackmail, perhaps. Because none of that is allowed in this business, you know. But, for whatever reason, it looks to us as though Kringle had to kill her, or have her killed. Then, he or somebody had to bury her, and what better place than the abandoned dump? But, then he panicked. So, a few days later—insofar as we can pin down the dates—he shot himself. Believe me, we've looked into all of this and I trust we've been, ah, decent and thorough about it. At any rate . . . so he had to kill himself for reasons known only to him. All the facts seem to point to him. Or, perhaps one of his so-called 'clients' had him killed, just in case the woman involved had . . . well, perhaps that is too complex for what looks like a relatively simple affair."

"But . . . but, wait up a minute. We found Glinda True's pocket-book on that body. And her ring. And the bus ticket. How do you figure all that shit in?"

"Oh, a mere detail, believe me. A plant, no doubt. We would not want to underestimate Kringle. Very clever, very clever. Very likely Kringle arranged to get hold of some false identification, plant it with the body, so if it were ever found, which was merely accidental, you understand, then it would appear to be Miss True herself, who, evidently, according to all testimony, her own in-cluded, made no secret of her desire to leave town with no inten-tion to return. Certainly as they were next-door neighbors, and him being an elderly man, she being an only child and no doubt a lonely girl, she might have turned to him for advice, and so forth. Therefore, he would have known about her plan to leave. Doubt-less, she knew nothing of this whatsoever. I must say, though this is strictly off the record, that she and her cousin, the elder Miss True, seem like perfect innocents to me. Just two women accidentally caught in the cross-fire, you might say."

"But . . . ," Gerald began.

"I'm nearly finished, and then I'd love to hear what you think about it. So, you see, we really do have it tied up. In fact, Miss True, both Misses True, have repeatedly told us the purse was stolen. It all adds up. In fact, rather neatly and quickly, I might add, as I've said." And Celted stood up, brushed off his pants, and turned to look down at Gerald who was still sitting, stunned, against the tree.

"Look, old boy, you've been super to work with. What I'll do is write this all up tonight and submit it and make sure you get a full report. You can do whatever it is you do with copies. This case is closed. Perhaps a few loose ends, of course. I mean, we'll probably never be able to determine just how the victim died, or exactly when, or, in fact, whose body it is, ah, was. So that's a little nagging. Unfortunate for our investigative purposes and skills, no matter how good they are, that the body was originally dumped where it was. I mean, naturally, buried where it was. As I see it— and my chief, incidentally, agrees with these conclusions—it's pretty cut and dried what took place. No missing person has ever been reported in the records of this town, and I can't believe you people would close ranks against justice like this, that is, if someone ever had been reported missing. So, if all this seems well, bizarre, unbelievable, believe me, this kind of, let's call it 'international crime' isn't new to me, just to, perhaps, you."

Gerald almost said "Fuck off." But he remembered it was Thanksgiving, and therefore almost Christmas. And the town needed to get on with its business. He, personally, needed to get on with the business of learning his lines. Jeez, he was Herod in this year's play, with more damn lines to learn than anybody else. Another reason to soften Yvonne up a little, so she'd help him at night by reading the other parts—the Angel, the Three Kings, the Messenger, and so forth. Of course she was making his costume, too, sewing some kind of stretchy gold stuff into a turban and putting some fuzzy furry stuff around the edges of his old robe. Looked pretty good, too. Something about Celted's theory bothered him, but he thought: why the hell not go along with it? This way, it's over with. Plus, it sounds logical enough. Maybe I can't see the trees for the forest, or however that goes. Anyhow, I think I'll just shut up now. Celted and his other uppy-ups would sure love a local deputy telling them how to run their business, anyhow.

"I always figured," Gerald said, getting up stiffly, "that old whatever he was was mixed up in this."

"I'm sure you did," Celted said. "I'm sure you did."

And I'm sure I didn't, thought Gerald, as they stumbled downhill towards the lights of the houses. I thought—what have I been thinking about this? I think I thought this was an inside job, with an inside motive. Whorehouses. Phooey. Bullshit. All of it. I was a lot younger than her, but I remember Glinda when she was around. That her pocketbook is found on that body is just too much of a coincidence for me.

I wouldn't put it past her, nor Adele neither, having been up to something. That Adele—the strong, silent type. But I bet they were involved, anyhow. These things just don't happen by themselves. If it weren't for something—but what is it?—I could buy this cockamamie theory of his. But there's something that bugs me. Whorehouses. Right. International yet. This was done by some-body good and pissed-off, that's what it was. Now, who that was, I'm not real clear. But I'm pretty sure it wasn't no . . . that's it! It couldn't have been Kringle that did it, like Celted says, because it couldn't have been a man at all! It's that pocketbook that bothers me, that's it. No man would think of doin' something that weird. That's a woman thinking about clues and such, a woman that's read too many goddamn books, mystery books. That's the kind of shit they do in mystery books. Plant something on the body. So, what kind of *man* reads *mystery* books? That's my point!

Well, what do I know? I do know one thing, though. If Yvonne ever was able to let go of this town, if we ever did leave. I mean, if I ever did get some fancy-dancy job in Boston or whatever, I don't think I'd move on a killing and get my mind all made up quite as fast as this. Not that I'm a bit sorry to have it over with. Don't get me wrong. I just think, that if I had Celted's job, I'd give it, I'm pretty goddamn sure, a better college try than this.

Chapter XIV

In Which Life Begins to Get Back to Normal
And Glinda Leaves Town at Last

We all know someone whose heart invariably skips a season ahead. For example, their Christmas shopping is done by July, wrapped and ready to be mailed by September in holiday paper they bought half price last January. In February, they go someplace hot where drinks are made with fresh coconuts. In a heat wave they warm up a beef stew in the microwave, but serve asparagus during a blizzard. They freeze quarts of strawberries and serve them in meringues on the darkest days of the year. Their air conditioning hums in May; their furnace clicks on the first chilly night in August. They wear light sweaters year-round and thin flat shoes, go to a tanning salon. In summer they buy sun oil with the highest possible SPF. Detailed plans for the Fourth of July are made in spring, and so forth. They might put up Valentine's Day trees, or Easter trees.

This mind is always preparing ahead, which can certainly be a useful thing, but when it rearranges the calendar it glosses over the event for which it prepared. This mind seems always ahead of the present moment, observing a calendar of sales rather than a calendar of events.

Sales—for example of Christmas paper in January—either come ahead of or follow ceremonies and times of year, and sales promise that we can have the next go-round at substantial savings. Thus, of course without being intended to do so, sales create the impression that ceremonies, like Christmas next year, are occasions for saving money. This subtly eliminates the old nature of ceremonies (or the times of year they mark) which was to spend lavishly, go for broke, eat the whole hog, kill the fattened goose, burn the biggest log, sacrifice the virgin, stick the finest blooms on graves, stick the best of the harvest into our gullets, and so on.

In addition to breaking down the old connection between time of year, religion, human activity, celebration, and cosmic fear, "sales" also give us a false sense of security. They never seem to take sudden or untimely death into account. Swimsuits go on sale when the nights turn nippy, coats when the days warm up. Perhaps even an odder kind of association is formed in our minds when "sales" of automobiles or mattresses celebrate the birth of an American President, thus suggesting that patriotism is also an opportunity to save money.

This particular mind is, very likely, suburban. The marketplace which creates its imagination is not one scruffy Country Store at a crossroads, but the endlessly potential mall. All town planners, if they have a human or Utopian bent, anyway, should understand that one central marketplace (square or store) creates a magnet, and it is by attraction that we live. Therefore, a general store (lunch counter, food, white gas, Blue Seal Feeds, milk, videos, beer and wine, news, bulletin board, etc.) resembles a lodge-pole, a cathedral, a town green, a sacred oak, a holy well, and so forth, much more than it resembles or is a forerunner or pathetic substitute for a large, up-to-date mall. What is a mall but the illusion of endless choices?

It doesn't make a lot of difference to this sacred and necessary organization of the daily, what is for sale at the Store. That is, take cans of mushrooms: if stems and pieces is all that's on the shelves, that's probably going to be all right. Not only because canned mushrooms more or less dissolve in any recipe anyhow, and so stems and pieces are going to be just as flavorful in the final dish, but because of all the goods the Store provides for which no shopper will ever pay a single dime.

News, and opinions of the day, for one thing. The real weather report, for another. The forum in which to throw a little tantrum in public, for another. (What is the good of a private snit?) The theater in which someone can perform in their bedroom slippers or sing a song about turkeys. Dear Storekeeper, you provide the arena where we can see anybody we know, get to snub them for a reason they will understand (and others will witness, and discuss). What's more, others will add the event onto our myth, as in, "Yeah, I saw Snooky at the Store. Do you b'lieve he was wearing those slippers of his? in this weather? and having a fit about mushrooms or some damned thing? What a weirdo. Well, takes all kinds, I guess, huh?" Thus a Store allows us to make history and also to accumulate one of our own.

Perhaps the most exquisite and complex pleasure is that the Store's various shortcomings ("sorry, outta slaw today, sorry about that") allow us to rail against the very thing that sustains us. In this sense, cursing the Store is tantamount to cursing God. Contempt breeds familiarity, which, if you think about it, is entirely to be desired. We long to be on close terms more than we long for the illusion of infinite freedom of choice. It's good and solid to know who's to blame. In this sense, Job's irate-customer-like relationship with God, as though Jehovah were a slap-dash inefficient proprietor behind the butcher counter, is much to be envied. That is, you can look Him right in the face and you know Him by name and you know what it is you were wanting that He doesn't have for you.

Therefore, to bitch about the Store—its eternal stems and pieces, its poisonous red hot dogs, its scruffy aisles full of nosy neighbors and white bread, its lukewarm over-boiled coffee, its lack of chicken livers when you need them—is a thing entirely good. It makes for thicker mental life, more engaged in the struggle at any rate, to bite the hand that feeds us than to gobble up, in servile fashion, at post-holiday sales, whatever leftovers of holiness or nature that hand decides to throw our way.

At the Store this morning, the week after Thanksgiving—Tuesday, to be exact—no one is bothering to pretend to drop in for a pint of molasses or a single onion, but is there early, to get the newspaper, hear the talk, add to the talk, grab a cup of and sit down, may as well. The headlines this morning announce: "Small Town's Halloween Murder Solved: Old International Crime Ring, Claim Experts."

No customer is without an opinion, and most utterances begin
with a shake of the head, some gesture of disbelief, relief, and superiority. (Who accustomed to malls, would even notice such theater, much less perform it? The wherewithal to notice or perform
takes a lifetime of practice, and practice takes place in the same
repeated spot: the bull's-eye target, the C scale, the hoop and net,
the fine-tuning of morals, ear to the instrument. Can't rush it.)

Thus the Store this morning is packed with messages, dense as
jam in a jar. "Well, whatever," is the general consensus. If the "experts" (Celted, lab technicians, etc.) anticipated awe, gratitude,
wonder, closure, agreement, or unschooled admiration of their ex-
pertise, then they are in for a disappointment. But the experts hoped
for none of these things, would not catch any nuance of the drama
anyway, and so are uniformly spared the disgrace that would
hound Gerald, for instance, were he responsible for solving the
crime and announcing his solution to the press. Murder solved?
Give us a break. Of course it isn't solved. Not the way I'd solve it.
Not like in the good old days. (Nor, perhaps, should it be solved.
To "solve" it would end the mystery, would end the talk and the
thinking, and that would be a terrible death. Better the murder is
kept alive. And in this endeavor, all the customers and coffee
drinkers this morning do their bit of sincere work.)

It's warmed up outside and is raining again. So the other topic
of Store talk is "Won't be a white Christmas at this rate." "Well,"
says someone, folding up the day's newspaper and fitting it back
into the sales rack, "well, at least we can get back to normal around
here." Whereupon a humorist replies, "Do you call Christmas without snow normal? Do you call rain at this time of year normal?
Guess *you* must be from away, huh?"

Across the wet messy street from the Store, in Adele's warm
kitchen, their heads close together for one of the few and certainly
the last time in their lives, Adele and Glinda read the headline and
story. "Well," says Adele. "Well," says Glinda, "that's over at least.
Not a bad story, really. I mean, they really did a good job of this!"

Next door Snooky is reading the paper aloud and yelling "International! International! Oh for heavens' sake, worldwide! Wide!

Spies or something! Now you remember when we bought this house! Remember who owned it before us? Yes you do. Just think! Remember a German they talked about? Well, him! No, he hasn't been arrested! He's been dead for years! Dead! The one they found dead in the dump is some business partner of his! Partner! Oh look, read it yourself. I'll be back in a minute. Got to check the pan. No! not a man! pan! pan! Here!" and Snooky thrust the newspaper onto Padre's lap and went to check the omelette. A headache already, and not even had breakfast yet. Well, back to normal! Back to normal! If you want to call this normal.

Puck got the news on his carphone, and drove to the Store. Harold overheard the news while waiting for his cup of free cocoa. Buzz got the newspaper in his mailbox at the dump gate. He read the headlines out loud, with Dog as audience. The school principal called an assembly in the cafeteria/all-purpose room, and announced the jist of the news and cautioned the pupils it was "over with now and so time to settle down and get back to work, no more funny stuff." The director of the Christmas Pageant bought the paper on his way home from the night shift at the mill, and thought: well, finally perhaps we can even have a halfway decent rehearsal. Though I doubt it. Yvonne hugged Gerald from behind while he was bent over the littered kitchen table reading, and said, "Honey, you did a hell of a job. How about taking the day off to do some Christmas for the kids?" Adele folded up the paper, put it in the woodbox, and thought of opening the shop one more time, but instead wrote out a sign and went across to tape it on the door: GONE FOR THE HOLIDAYS—OPEN AFTER THE FIRST. She returned home and started to pack, make lists, and do some phone calling.

"Darling, do I have to tell you more than one time? Of course I don't mind! I'm happy for you! And I don't want you to think of me for one minute, do you hear me? Not for one single minute. More sherry? Of course I won't 'be lonely' all by myself. And this back thing I've got—it's nothing, just a twinge of some kind. If it gets worse, well, toodle-dee-doo. And this cough? Nothing. Of *course* I can handle doing costumes by myself. How many in the cast. Twenty-four, not counting the children? Believe me, Adele, I *want* you to go. I *insist* that you go. Don't be ridiculous. Naturally, I'll miss you. Who wouldn't? For that matter, so will the Library Tea committee, but I'm sure we can find someone to fill in for you. It won't be the same, but whoever said Christmas has to be the same year after blessed year? Kick up your heels for once! I know I would. That is—sandwich?—if I could ever ever get away, ever, which I very much doubt, things as they are."

Thus Snooky did his best to console Adele. Adele tried to console Snooky by hiding her pleasure over the coming trip, by eating several more sandwiches of anchovy paste than she wanted, and by drinking two glasses of sherry, which she didn't like all that much. She said to herself she'd bring him back *two* presents, and a little treat for the Padre, too.

"Let's have a . . . what could we have?" she asked. "A tea party soon as I get back? Whatever, Snooky, promise not to take the tree down, promise? And promise to remember every detail of the Library Tea, and who came, and what they brought. I swear, if Yvonne brings those lemon squares one more time I want you to tell me about it."

"Darling, I won't miss a beat, believe me. And I'll be gentle breaking your news to the Old Relic. He *is* used to Christmases all together, you know, and might kick up a fuss. He'll want to know why you've left, and I'll have to scream my brains out explaining, but I'm sure I can do it. Of course he's apt to be upset the whole time you're gone, but Darling, that's all right. If he could only comprehend, I know he'd want you to have a good time."

Adele licked her forefinger and picked up the crumbs from her lap and ate them. She looked at the half-trimmed tree in front of her, at the unwrapped ornaments on the rug, at Snooky's reindeer cookies on the plate, at the sprigs of boxwood on the mantle, the red candles, the color photo of the Queen. She thought of the piles of starched, ironed, clean clothes on her bedroom chair, of the open brown suitcase, of the ride down the highway, of the lights of Boston.

"Well, I must go home. I'll be back, you know, sooner than you think. And you must tell me all, and we'll have a party, and make some plans for fun things this spring. We've really been getting into a rut, you know, and we're not getting any younger, you and me! Let's make a plan to do all the things we keep saying we'll do, come spring. Like take a wildflower walk, or transplant those white iris. That is, unless you decide to take a trip to San Francisco!"

"Oh, I can just see *me* getting away! Now look, Darling, you have a delicious time. I'll fetch Fido first thing in the morning, take care of the keys, make sure everything's all right at your house, and wish you a bon voyage. And a Merry Christmas, to boot. Now, out you go. Not to think of a thing! Not me, not frozen pipes, not the Padre, not Christmas dinner, not the Library Tea, not the Pageant, not a thing, promise?" And good Snooky saw Adele down his porch steps, waved good-bye, watched her cross his yard into her own, go in her door, and he didn't go back into his own kitchen until he saw her kitchen lights go on.

Two slips, 3 skirts, 2 sweaters, 4 pair hose, 1 robe, boots, Fido's dish, change bed, vitamins, call post office (scratched through), vitamins for Fido, coat, cards? Wear 1 slip, take one. Dress? Pipes. Harold's headdress, play. Call *today*. Nightgowns, 2? Robe. Shoes. What about clothes on a cruise?

Oh, heavens, begin another list. Summer suit? White shoes? (Ask Glinda.) Harold's headdress. Baby Jesus doll. Put on list: headdress. Jesus doll. Straw for manger, where? Oil man. Angel wings. Let's see: 1 slip, sweaters, robe.

"Adele! Adele! What in *hell* are you doing up there? Solving the world problems? Look, leave most of that junk here, if you're packing again. We'll go on a shopping spree soon as we hit town! You could use some new things, God knows, okay? Adele? Now come on down and have some supper and let's get to bed for a change, get on the road, okay? Adele?"

"Packing," shouted Adele, "packing. Be down in a minute. Go ahead and set the table if you will."

I've got more set than that my friend, thought Glinda, slamming unmatched plates and two cups on the table. One more of these meals, and that's it for me. But stay cool, stay cool. Almost home. Marc, you big boy, you! God, did I ever miss *you*! Did oo miss me, just a widdo bit? Oh, a touch of skiing, some family business with lawyers, a few little hometown holiday doings, but thought of you the whole time, you doll, you. My drag of a cousin was going to come, she's quite elderly, you know, and that held me up, but thank God, at the last minute, she just couldn't tear herself away from country life. Well, she isn't in that good a health anymore. And the country is quaint, I'll admit that much, and I miss it a bit, you know? I mean, it really does look just like a Christmas card. Saw all my old friends, well, those who didn't have the brains to get out. But, Poopy-Doops, enough about me. Now, what shall we do for Christmas? Tell Gwinda something you would twooly twooly kill for.

"Adele? Ready! Come *on*, for Christ sake. It'll get cold!" and Glinda kicked the cat, hard, then rattled a pot lid to cover up its cries.

Their plan is to leave at 7:00 A.M., sharp. Everything is ready. Adele's brown suitcase stands near the back door. The key, food for Fido, and various notes are on the kitchen table for Snooky. The sink is empty. All committees have been called, all responsibilities absolved. The green shades are pulled, the fire is dying down, the African violets are watered one last time. Tired from the efforts to think of every detail, and from the excitement, Adele goes to sleep as soon as her head hits the pillow.

In her bed downstairs, Glinda lay on her back and stared up at the invisible ceiling. God, this room is like a Christly coffin.

Adele is not very good at planning things because she has never needed to plan much. Glinda is not good at planning because she has never been responsible for much. A large quotient of belief in "luck," "chance," and "other people might take care of the boring stuff, but not me" plus a profound conviction that everyone else was very stupid and so would never guess, or know, or catch her, has always caused Glinda's plans to remain sketchy, impulsive, fuzzy. She wants to murder Adele—in fact, within a few hours—

and get the money and have (buy) Marc. To her mind, these are the essential facts. Everything else is mere details.

Beyond these facts—murder Adele, get Marc—everything else resembles a slipshod, low-budget movie set. Glinda can only see herself as the star, not the producer, not the director, and certainly not all the minor types who take care of boring details. Glinda is above details because she has desire; or, because she has a vision.

She has a vision of murder in mind, but has no idea of the weapon or place or means or possible consequences. She lives nearly in downtown Boston, on a fifth floor, but has not thought of what to do with a 176-pound corpse. She would not remember to buy food for Fido, or tell the post office what to do with her mail, and things like that. It doesn't occur to her to get a story ready for the lawyers, nor does it occur to her that lawyers tend not to believe stories. She knows deep down that Marc is a nit, but thinks a red car and some love will change his character. Her thinking happens in simple sentences: I want money. I will kill Adele. I will have the money. Marc will marry me. Screw the details. As for feelings of remorse—no, she doesn't fret about that at all.

If the mind is a room, if we can imagine that, and if we can imagine that thoughts have literal shape and size, then Marc is larger than anything else in her head. He is like an Abyssinian stone god at the gates of her city. Blood sacrifice, self-immolation, blind obedience, intense but mindless busyness—all mere details compared to the need to worship. All and everything can get tossed on the reeking altar. Her life, Adele's life, Snooky's life, the thoughts and ties and dependencies of the town, each and all connections, the life to come—all this is general blood, general wine to be poured at the clawed feet of the blind stone god. The god himself, tonight, several hundred miles south, lets his hand just grace Traci's thigh, just for a second, under the table at the bar. To Marc, it's a beneficent gesture, one which he wants Traci to take as meaningful, one that will completely satisfy her and get her off his case. Alas, Traci is no fool, has zero religious impulse, and will soon be laughing with her roommates about Marc and his icky ways.

Flat on her back, staring up into darkness, Glinda comes up

with an idea. She needs, she decides, one really solid witness. To the murder? Ah, of course not. To her feelings. Specifically, to her feelings of being overjoyed that Adele is coming to Boston with her. That they will have a family Christmas, and all that cha-cha-cha. That her mission (come home, visit, take care of Adele, etc.) is accomplished.

Snooky would be the perfect witness to this, but she can sense his recoil and disbelief. Not good. That is, not useful. Harold of course is out. Gerald—well, she doesn't even really know Gerald, so no pull there. The old preacher? Ridiculous. Who is left? Buzz! Buzz could be her witness. He'd always believed everything she'd ever told him, was such a sucker, so why not now?

Therefore, how to see Buzz at the last minute, just before leaving town? Too bad she didn't have this inspiration last night, before it got so late. I'll just pop in, tell him good-bye, tell him how glad I am Adele's coming with me, promise to write him often, kiss him for old time's sake. I'll pat the dog, tell Buzz how much he's always meant to me. Buzz himself, not the fucking dog. Someday, just in case something might go wrong, which I doubt, and I need somebody to say something or other to back me up, well, Buzz'll be the one to do it. He'll say, "Yip, she came to see me just afore her and Adele left town, told me how glad she was Adele was getting a vacation, how much it meant to both of them, so nice to see them two girls gettin' together again after all this while." When she made up his lines in her head (forgetting that Buzz does not speak this way at all), Glinda was convinced that this was exactly, word for word, what Buzz would say. To invent his purpose was to create his reality.

It was all pretty simple. She'd get up an hour earlier than she'd planned and walk up to his little house on the far side of the dump. She'd have to wake him up, she supposed, but he'd probably think that was kind of cute and typical. "Woke me up crack of dawn, she did, just to personally tell me good-bye. Course she was always different than most folks, always up to sumpin'."

She dozed a little. Outside, the rain stopped. She woke with a start. Nearly 6:00, perfect. Go see Buzz right now. She got out of bed, took off her nightgown, stuffed it in her bag, pulled the covers up over the warm sheets, put on her traveling outfit—red slacks, red sweater, her boots. Looked around the room to see if she'd missed anything, decided she hadn't, zipped her carryall, turned off the bedside table lamp. In the dark kitchen she thought: what if Adele wakes up and finds me gone? I don't want her to freak out now. I'd better leave a note. "Gone to tell Buzz g-bye. Be right back," she wrote on a pad and propped it against the kettle where Adele would be sure to see it. Though, of course, she'd probably get back before Adele was even up.

She put her carryall on the floor alongside Adele's old suitcase, and quietly let herself out the backdoor. She crossed the street and started up the hill towards the dump. It was still dark, and the wet streets shone in the orangy glow of the mercury arc lamps. The town slept. A light on here and there, but utterly quiet. The smell of rain, of mud, of smoldering overnight stove fires.

Glinda climbed over the broken fence and entered the dump ground. The sky was turning gray. The one dead tree in the center of the dump stood like a skeleton against the eastern sky. A rooster crowed three times. Get this over with, girl, get this over with. She trudged upwards, skirting the burn piles, could see the outline of Buzz's little sleeping house on the far side, like a crayon drawing. What a life, she thought. He should've stuck with me, forgetting for the moment that she'd been the one to scrape him off like a barnacle stuck to a prow.

The huge eyes suddenly flared to her right, and the hot, strong, panting body jumped against her, nearly knocking her down on the filth, the crap, the broken bits and pieces of a thousand lives. "Jesus Christ! What the hell!" But it was only Dog, on his dawn patrol, who recognized a friend when he smelled one. "Jesus Christ, get the fuck off, would you?" It was so cold and the encounter had so frightened her that Glinda could not feel that her hair was standing on end, nor could she register her own harsh and rapid breath, nor tell that she'd broken out in a soaking sweat. "Christ," she kept saying, brushing off her outfit, "Christ Almighty, let me outta here."

Dog put his tail between his legs and slunk back into his bed on the seat of Earth Angel, Buzz's backhoe.

Glinda stood there for a minute, trying to catch her breath. Had she been able to look in a mirror, she would have seen her face pale as a ghost. She held her hand against her chest (that unconscious family gesture) and turned and looked through the smoking piles of rubbish and junk down to the low-lying town. It was just visible, looked like an art postcard. A few more kitchen or barn lights were on. Smoke from newly-raked fires went straight up into the pale, silent air. "Whoo-eee," said Glinda out loud, "whoo-eee! Good-bye hellhole at last!"

Dog, hearing her jubilant "whoo-eee," decided she had forgiven him. She's playing a game, he thought, so I'll do my part, too. He jumped up and down on the seat and flipped around and thumped his tail and in his excess of joy and early-morning energy accidentally threw his entire weight against the old gear shift, enough to kick it into neutral. The machine lurched a few feet, stopped, lurched again. Already tilted on the incline, its wheels began to crunch forward. A ride, too! thought Dog. What a good game!

Earth Angel, silent as its name, heavy as a god, gathered speed down hill. Glinda couldn't hear it coming. She turned to resume her climb, and was too surprised and disbelieving to move out of the way. It easily knocked her flat and without pause rolled onwards. It didn't stop until it came onto level ground and up against the broken fence at the bottom of the hill, nearly right out into the road, as someone at the Store said later that morning. Right out into the road, could've killed more than one at that rate, said someone else. Everyone nodded. I've been tellin' and tellin' the Selectmen, said another, it was time for some up-to-date equipment up to that dump. Goddamn shame, said someone else, but I guess we're lucky, if you know what I mean. That it didn't roll right out into traffic.

Chapter XV

In Which the Town Gets Ready for Christmas

Whatever the police did with the bones found in the dump on Hallowe'en night, no one ever asked. An unmarked grave possibly, beyond the pale. Glinda was buried in the pink-lined casket, with another tasteful graveside service, this time done quite briefly by the Baptist minister who used neither bell, book, nor candle. For the second time in little more than a month, the whole town came to her funeral. The envelope, "In Memory of Glinda True," went back up on the cash register at the Store. There was enough for several decorated wreaths, some pots of white mums, and Snooky sent tall pink gladiolas which shriveled and died in the cold before the final graveside prayer had been said. "A fine funeral, again," someone said afterwards. "We can get back to normal, I guess."

Single-handedly, Snooky managed to waylay the benefit bean supper on the grounds that "enough, ladies, is enough." There was no one who didn't agree with that sentiment. Because nearly two weeks still remained before the Christmas pageant, the director and his committee and the cast had a meeting (before rehearsal) and decided to go ahead with it, despite "this sad business." Gerald, wearing his Herod costume to get used to walking in a skirt, suggested that Santa Claus (Puck), who was also Master of Ceremonies this year, could add a few words to his welcoming speech about Glinda's death—or, "this sad time"—as everyone was calling it. Puck could add something about the whole town sticking together and getting through "this sad time" and coming out the other side better people who counted their blessings every day, especially at Christmas. Did everyone agree this was the right touch? Everyone agreed, and they had a good rehearsal with nearly all the minor characters off the book, and only three people still needing help with finding their costumes.

After a few days of mourning and business, Adele took down the sign and opened the shop, whereupon she sold nearly everything in stock because everyone wanted to "support" her and also because they wanted to see how she was doing.

How was she doing? She'd gotten up the morning of the trip, pulled her covers up over her warm sheets, dressed in her traveling clothes, gone downstairs to make tea, and found Glinda's note. She made tea, waited. Waited. Had the darkest thoughts. Made more tea. Watched the clock. Walked through all the cold rooms one more time. Felt in the dirt of the African violets. Came back to the kitchen, sat and waited. Thought of phoning someone, but didn't know what for. Watched the clock. Saw Glinda's bag all packed. Waited. Reread the note. Was thinking of calling Snooky when, around 7:30, Buzz drove into her driveway and parked behind Glinda's red car, got out, and walked towards the backdoor.

Since then, all things had repeated themselves: the phone calls, the potato salads, the sponge cakes, Snooky's fussing over sandwiches, Gerald returning to the liquor store for more sherry, the expensive coffin getting moved from police headquarters back to the funeral home, the wreaths, the ride home, the funeral lunch.

"Makes you think," she said to Snooky next day. "Just makes you think."

"It does indeed, Old Sweetheart. That it does. Ah, well, we must try to pull ourselves together, be merry in spite of, don't you agree? Life must go on, you know, it just must."

"Snooky, I've been thinking. I had made up my mind—before all this happened, I mean—to buy Glinda a few, well, presents. I've got a bit of money saved you know, or maybe not, but I'd decided to spend a bit of it improving things around here when I got back, too. From my trip. And honestly, what do you think? I see no reason, as things stand, and you're right we're not getting any younger, not to go ahead with those plans. What do you think?"

"Oh, Precious, *what*? Oh tell!"

"Well," Adele warmed to the subject, "I'd thought of putting in a new bathtub, for one. And getting the house painted, for another. Fixing up the shop a little, adding an addition, even. You know I've always wanted a bookshop, or, I mean, wanted to sell books, too. This is no spur-of-the-minute idea, Snooky, I wouldn't want you to think I was just throwing away money without giving it a lot of thought. Anyhow, I think, come spring, I'll look into this, get some bids and all. Glinda, bless her, was going to help me choose a few new things to wear, so I see no reason why I shouldn't go ahead and do that, too. I know it might sound strange, but it would feel good if I used the money I'd budgeted to spend on some presents for her to buy myself a few things. She'd have liked that, I know. What do you think?"

"Oh, Precious, she would! She would *want* you to. You know, Adele, she really was a nicer person than you told me she was. Now I'm not saying you had a bad attitude, Darling, or anything like that. But I could tell she had a good heart, underneath. A bit rough around the edges, but look at it this way: she just didn't have your advantages, did she? And I could tell she had real affection for you, too. As who, Precious Friend, would not? Of *course* she'd want you to spend that money on yourself."

"Oh, I was hoping you'd agree. I also need your help doing a good deed. You said you'd go with me in the spring to pick out a headstone for Glinda. Well, do you think we could see if the monument people could also make a nice marker, maybe a bronze plaque or something along those lines? Do you think they do that sort of thing?"

"I'm sure they do; Gerald would know. But why would you want a headstone *and* a plaque, Sweetheart?"

"Oh, not both for Glinda. The headstone for her grave. But I thought perhaps some little sort of memorial for the person who was buried in the dump. I talked to Wilma about it, and she thought something like that would look very appropriate in the pines on the north side of the Library, or even on the walk right below Shakespeare's bust. We don't know her name or who she was, exactly, so it would have to be simple—In Memory of an Unknown Visitor—something like that. And then I thought, in addition, of giving Wilma or the Trustees a certain amount of money each year specifying that they spend it on art books. What do you think?"

Snooky was wiping his eyes and blowing his nose loudly into a big blue handkerchief. "Honestly. Honestly. Too lovely. I don't know what to say. Who else would have thought of it?"

"Now, one more thing. Don't laugh at me, promise? Something I've always wanted. Well, two things. Snooky, I've always longed to have a cockatiel, in a fancy big cage, something to keep Fido and me company in the kitchen. And the other day, when you and Gerald and I were shopping, I saw one in the pet shop window at the mall. Just the one I've always wanted. Now, you promised!"

"Darling Thing, I'm *not* laughing. I'm just delighted! What fabulous plans! But what's the second funny thing, you said '*two*'? And let's call Gerald at once, want to?"

"The other thing is—now don't laugh—to invite you to dinner. Not you and the Padre and Buzz and all, just you. A nice little dinner, you and me. I'll cook for you for a change. Would you come?"

"Precious, come? But of course I would come! Name the date! Give me time to brush off my best suit! What can I bring?"

"Not a single thing, Snooky. Not one single thing. You'll be my guest for a change."

"My," said Snooky, taking a sip of tea and trying to hide his dismay behind his cup. What *would* she make him eat? Sardines on toast? Jello? Boiled carrots? Beans from that disgraceful filthy bean pot? "Paint. Bathtubs. Bookshop. New clothes. Art books. Dinner invitations. A bird in a cage. We *are* having a second childhood, aren't we?"

"Not exactly," said Adele. "More like a first."

A few days later, on the Friday evening before Christmas on Monday, Snooky is shaving. His suit is laid out on the bed. He pats his face in the mirror, pats on some cologne, winces. He's had Gerald buy a bouquet in town, and he managed to find a nearly drinkable wine at the Store. He writes out a white card: "To A. from S., The Merriest—" then thinks better of that possibility under the circumstances, and writes a new card: "To A. from S., Always," and sticks it between two pink carnations. He wraps the bottle of wine in tissue paper and struggles with the bow. Heavens, he thinks, what will be next?

Over at her house, Adele turns the oven down low and goes upstairs to the bathroom to touch up her rouge and repowder her forehead. In a cookbook of Gram's she found a recipe called "Oven Dinner," and that is what she has cooked. It looks and smells lovely. A large chuck roast, first. Rub in some flour, brown both sides in hot fat, place in heavy oven-proof dish with 1 envelope onion soup mix, 1 can mushroom soup, 1 can water. Cook 4 to 5 hours, covered tightly. Two hours before serving, add 4 peeled potatoes, cut into chunks.

She has done all this, plus arranged canned pear halves on iceberg lettuce and added several heaping spoons of mayonnaise to each, then sprinkled shredded store cheese on top. Then she put both salads in the woodshed to stay cool.

The table in the dining room looks beautiful: a white cloth, two white napkins, two matching plates, two blueberry-scented candles in Gram's old silver candlesticks. Adele has on a new tan sweater and a new gray skirt. She powders her forehead, drags a comb through her tight new perm, goes downstairs to open a bottle of Chablis. Luckily, as she owns no corkscrew, the bottle of wine has a pry-off lid. She puts the open bottle of wine on the table next to the candles, glances at the clock—half an hour left—and sits down.

She thinks of turning on the 5:30 news, but instead just sits there, looking out the steamed-up window and listening to the recorded chimes from the church steeple—"O Holy Night"—followed by "Ave Maria." We must, she thinks, urge them to get a new tape next year. Perhaps that's something Snooky and I could contribute to. I'll have to remind myself to discuss it with him. We can talk about it over dinner. She gets up and lights the blue candles. It's snowing in time for Christmas. All around her house and all over town, the snow falls gently in big flakes and the recorded chimes play the Christmas songs. Just like on cards, the candles on Adele's dinner table make little round glows through the frosty windows.

Harold, walking by, thinks it looks very seasonal. He's on his way next door to baby-sit Father Kildare. Snooky has told him that Father would be fed, ready for bed, in his pajamas, wanting to watch the news, and all Harold has to do is keep him company and keep an eye out. Harold nodded, thought he could do that. "I'll only be right next door," Snooky had explained, "but I'd feel so much better if you were here just in case." Harold nodded. He understood. "And count on having supper here, too . . . which would be such a blessing," Snooky added. "That way, I won't have to worry about any of you." Harold nodded.

He rapped at Snooky's back door which was immediately yanked open by Snooky himself. Gosh, thought Harold, a bow tie, and his suit, and flowers, and gosh, he smells like perfume! There was supper on a tray on the table. Something in gravy, with little squinchy bits of parsley on top, and another little white oval dish with steamy potatoes and buttery runlets, and then a custard cup, looked like, with something chocolatey-looking and a fat spoon of cream on top. A napkin. The Ritz, thought Harold, the Ritz. Which meant "fancy," he knew that.

"Your salad's in the fridge," said Snooky, "and the Padre's had his dins, and he's in there watching the news and looking so forward to your visit. Let's let him think it's a visit, okay? Just a visit. But you take your tray in there and keep him company. Now remember, I'm just next door. If a thing goes wrong, call me. Well, no. Never mind. Just run over. Now, he might want some hot Ovaltine. Turn the burner until you hear the click, then turn it down. When the milk almost boils, but not quite, here's the Ovaltine. Put in some of this cream. Oh, heavens. Wait. Ah, here's the cream. Put in a smidge of cream, he loves that. Make sure he gets to the men's room before he goes nigh-nigh, okay? Now call me—I mean, come over—if something goes wrong. Oh, I must rush. Will you be all right?"

Gosh, thought Harold, sure I'll be all right. He nodded and nodded, held his tray in both hands, waited for Snooky to leave. Snooky looked around anxiously, picked up the bouquet, the bottle of wine, put them both down, wrapped a white muffler around his neck, checked Harold's tray, got the salad out of the fridge and made room for it on the tray, picked up the bouquet, the bottle of wine, his gloves, and, worried looking, went out the backdoor. Harold waved good-bye with the fingers of one hand.

He kicked open the hall door as he had seen Snooky do so many times and headed towards the sound of the TV. In the front parlor the old priest sat in his pajamas and robe and slippers, a blanket around his shoulders, a blanket around his legs, watching the weather report. Pussums lay sleeping at his feet.

The room was lit by an enormous Christmas tree in the bay window. Stacks of presents were under the tree, all wrapped so pretty. Harold wanted to see which stack was his, but knew he shouldn't peek yet. Father Kildare looked up happily as Harold came in, motioned him to pull up a footstool, and turned up the sound.

"Sorry, folks," the weatherman was saying, "I'm afraid it's a bad old day tomorrow. This cloud right here" (and he pointed behind him to a moving pulsating thing in the middle of the map of the country) "means maybe up to four or as much as six inches of that nasty stuff, I hate to tell you."

The nice TV lady watching the weatherman laughed but said "Ouch!" And the weatherman laughed and said, "I wish I could promise you something nice," and she said, "Give us a break!" and laughed again, and the weatherman laughed and said, "I think one is coming." Harold wondered what they were talking about. Some more snow would just make everything more Christmasy. But then, maybe not where they lived.

He pulled up his footstool, sat down, balanced his supper tray on his knees, and picked up his spoon to eat his dessert first. From the steeple the slow tinkle of "Oh, Little Town of Bethlehem" mixed up with the falling blobs of snow. On the tree in the big window, the bubble lights bubbled and the tinsel twinkled, all green, and yellow, and red, and pink, against the deep blue of the night.

"Well," said the pretty TV lady, "Can you order some of this snow in a few days? I'm looking forward to a white holiday, at least!"

"Gosh," Harold said in his head, "I love Christmas."

"Me, too, " said Father. Harold smiled knowingly.

"Well, so, Father," he thought, looking up from his dessert, "so what would you like to talk about tonight?"

THE END